THE WINNERS CIRCLE, GAINING SUCCESS
GOD'S WAY

A Novel by Shawn Renard Mosley

Copyright © 2014 by Purple Diamond Publishing

Published by Purple Diamond Publishing LLC

First Edition

Facebook:
https://www.facebook.com/shawn.mosley.965?fref=
ts

Cover design/Graphics: Ben Harris Jr.

1

Dedication

I dedicate this book to my two beautiful

Daughters, Shawndrea and Joy Marie

Mosley.

I also dedicate this book to my mother, Patricia George

I am thankful to my niece, Melissa George,

For helping me with this work

And making the printing of this book

Possible.

AND, OF COURSE, TO GOD, I GIVE ALL

THE GLORY!

Table of Contents

THE PROBLEM WITH PEOPLE PLEASER

Chapter 1

Obviously, I am not trying to win the approval of people, but of God. If pleasing people were my goal, I would not be Christ's servant. Galatians 1:10 (NLT)

Some of the most frustrated people in the world are men pleasures. You will find that these types of people have strong insecurity problems. They go out of their way to gain some acceptance. The main reason for their frustration is that they easily put themselves under the control of others. They act how they feel others expect them to act. This makes men pleasers master role players. If these types of people are offended, they will not say anything sometimes about the offense because they do not want to hurt anybody's feelings.

These people try to say all of the right words at the right time. They try to do everything that others expect them to do. In most cases, they compromise their own morals and values. Men pleasers do not necessarily go along with what is right but that which is popular. Some people have played so many different roles trying to please others until they now have identity crises. In other words, they no longer know themselves.

One of the most dreadful things in the world is for a person to exist without identification of one's self. Men pleasers are not drivers in life but they are always someone's passenger. They live their entire life riding on someone else's coat tails. I have also discovered that men pleasers are driven people. The mere fact that they want to make everybody happy, they find themselves going out of their way to appease others.

Men pleasers could have good ideas and dreams, but if one person disapproves of their dreams, then that's enough to kill it simply because that other person was not pleased with it.

Living under the conscious thoughts of someone else's opinions and expectations must be a miserable way to live. God invites us back to life through the above scripture. By winning God's approval, we discover a better quality of life and freedom. When we make it, our goal to please God He in return shows us who we were created to be. Pleasing God sometimes goes against the grain of what is popular. The man who dares to please God fully will sometimes find himself walking alone.

Knowing God as our creator, he alone knows what is best for us. He has given us instruction in His book (The Bible) on how He expects us to live. These instructions are not given to us so that God could be some kind of tyrant over us. But He knows that in pleasing Him we find peace, joy, and liberty.

Whenever we live our lives as men pleasers, we find ourselves interested in worshiping the creation more that the Creator, since the word worship means the one who we are willing to fully surrender ourselves to. If you are ever going to be successful in this lifetime, then you have got to pull yourself from under the shadow of what people think about you. Any worthwhile accomplishments that you will have in this life will depend highly upon your confidence level, which is a result of one who pleases God.

If your inner self is not in tact then the manifestation of your outer life will be in disarray also. God will even alter the hearts of people around you and even those who don't like you when you please Him.

Proverbs 16:7 says, when a man's ways please the Lord, He maketh even his enemies to be at peace with him.

In order to be successful in life you need the favor of others. This type of favor does not come by kissing up to men but by loving on God. Another way that we please God is through the Avenue of Faith.

Hebrews 11:6 Without faith it is impossible to please God.

Men pleasers trust in what men can do for them but God pleasers trust in Him and are not disappointed. It pleases God when you put your trust and hope in Him as your source. God does not want to come second to none. If you have dreams and plans of success, the only way that you will be able to obtain those dreams is when you are delivered from the opinions of others. It is ok to be different. You don't have to fit into anyone else's opinions of who you are. You do not need anyone to validate you, all that matters is that God accepts you and you accept yourself.

Your success depends on two things, you listening to God and Him giving you direction. God always speaks to His children. You may say how can I hear God? There is always three ways that God speaks. I like to call them the powerful W's. Which are the witness, word and the way. These powerful W's are better understood in the life of the Christian who has a prayer life. The first way that God will talk through you is through His Word. But without prayer, even the Word does not stand out for your own situation.

Then there is the inward witness when you have a consistent prayer life, God will speak to your Spirit and guide you. The last way for you to know when God is speaking to you is He will open up the way for you to accomplish whatever task or blessing He is trying to get you to do or understand. Men pleasers make time for people but God pleasers make time for God. Who has the most influence over your life? You cannot be a servant of Christ if you are a man pleaser. Men pleasers are more interested in pleasing people than they are Christ. Even if

9

Christ were to give them direction, if it goes against popular opinion, they will not obey it. God could use His Apostles so mightily because they learned not to let people dictate to them how they should live and preach but they followed the Spirit of Christ.

On this journey that we are about to take together, I had to start it out by letting you know that you have got to drop off the opinions and influence that people have over you. Without first breaking down that wall then the rest of the principles that we share will be in vain. It takes boldness to walk away from the opinions of others.

Jeremiah 1:8 NLT And don't be afraid of the people, for I will be with you and will protect you...

The root cause of men pleasing is fear and we will deal with that in more detail in another chapter.

GIVE YOURSELF SOME TIME

Chapter 2

I returned, and saw under the sun, that the race is not to the swift, nor the battle to the strong, neither yet bread to the wise, nor yet riches to men of understanding, nor yet favor to men of skill; but time and chance happeneth to them all. Ecclesiastes 9:11 (KJV)

If I can stress one thing to you about the accomplishment of your dreams, it would be summed up in these two words. "Stay diligent." The most qualified or talented does not always get the job. Although gifts, talents, and abilities are important, it is not nearly as important as your diligence and your persistence. Whatever you commit to the blessing is found in staying with it until you see it unfold. Prepare for the season of your success. If you stay ready when your time comes, you will not have to get ready.

Finding one thing in life that you can dedicate yourself to will eventually bring you success if you stay with it. If you only stay persistent in something then you will find yourself in a life that is full and productive. Most people give up because they are more conscience with a time frame than the dream itself. There must be a season of endurance before the dream comes to pass. The word ENDURANCE means to continue; to bear up, as under pain.

When it comes down to the fulfillment of your dream it does not matter how painful it gets you must continue to focus on that in which you are trying to accomplish. There will be times when things will get so hard but you must never stop trying. There are people who are very talented and gifted and if only they could have held on and kept pressing forward then they could have seen their dreams come to pass. But instead of pushing forward, they gave up.

6

In the season of endurance. Dig deep, pull out your most worthy fight, and be willing to stay with the fight until the dream manifests. There are those who are less talented and not half as gifted as others but they have broken down the levies of struggle with endurance and not they are experiencing the floods of success. Remember that there is no such thing as failure until you decide to stop trying.

Temporary set backs are not intended to cause you to give up. The reasons for the setbacks are for you to reassess your method of accomplishing you intended goals. Do not let your temporary setback frustrate you. Look for new angles and approaches in how to accomplish your dreams.

CHANGE YOUR PERSPECTIVE: CHANGE YOUR LIFE

<u>A man becomes who he thinks he is from the heart.</u>

It is amazing that everything that your life has become up to this point is a result of how you perceive life. Your perception determines the outcome of you failures and successes. Self-encouragement will change your perception. What is the difference between the man who lives in extreme poverty and the man who enjoys wealth and riches? In both cases, it has to do with how they each think. One man thought his way to wealth while the other, his way to poverty and lack.

If you are not in the place in life that you want to be then it is only because you are not thinking right. Change you thinking and you will change your outcome and over all destiny.

It was your best or worst thinking that got you to where you are in life. True happiness, wealth, success and yes even good health are a result of how we think. You will never change anything about your current condition unless you are first willing to humbly admit that there is something mentally wrong with the way that your life has turned out.

Now this is not to say that you are crazy but it does mean that your mental choices are off course to where you want your life to end up. Clear mental direction and knowledge of one's self will always end up in success. If you are confused about who you are and where you are going then do not expect anyone else to tell you. You must learn to get an honest and clear

Definition of self. This includes knowing your strengths and weaknesses. Only when you define yourself can you believe in yourself. You cannot have a strong belief in anyone that you do not even

17

know, even yourself. By believing in yourself, you also believe in the God who made you.

God has made inside of you everything that is needed to make you a success. You will find out that most people who do not believe in themselves do not have much faith in God either. Believe it or not, how you view life is a matter of choice. Everybody in this world has faced obstacles and difficulties. It is a matter of how you perceive these obstacles that determines the outcome. The scenario that I am trying to make is when you look at the glass of water that has been poured to the half way mark do you see it as half empty or half full?

Actually, it can be either; it depends on how you perceive it. This depends on a matter of negative or positive thinking. Your mind is like a computer that has been programmed with

much data both negative and positive. The person who has been down loaded with much negative information always ends up viewing life from a negative aspect. Not only can you program your mind to do things that have brought countless others success and happiness, but the mind is so powerful until it can cause you to accomplish things that have never been done before.

Throughout history, mankind has thrived on doing things that were at one point thought to be impossible. Before the Wright Brothers invented the airplane, many people thought that the very idea of man defying gravity was insane. But there was something in the minds of the

Wright Brothers that challenged them to go beyond all limitations and make the impossible possible. Because the Wright Brothers did not allow themselves to be conformed to someone else's limitations and opinions of what they were capable of, today airplanes take us all over the world in record-breaking time. All of this started from the mind of men with a good idea. We must realize that the mind that God gave us is very powerful and the only limitations that you have are those that you place on yourself.

Our whole existence and outlook on how we view life is a direct result of how we think. Most of the mental bondage and torment that we experience in life is because we do not down load our minds with truth. Any area of our live that truth is not known then a lie has the opportunity to dominate and deceive us. Have you ever stopped to think that many of the negative thoughts that you experience are a result of lies that were seemingly forced upon you? The problem with believing lies is, if you believe them long enough then they will become your reality. All things become possible when you believe them.

We have got to take a second look at certain things that we have allowed to be a part of our belief system. Out truths are a result of our parents, teachers, relatives, pastors, religions and others who have had influence in our lives. Although some of what we hold, as truth cannot be argued such as when the sun shines it is daylight and when the stars shine it is night. Most truth can be argued depending upon where we get it from. Truth has its own voice and in time, it will speak for itself. The end result of truth is always liberation and freedom.

The reason for failure, mental torment, depression, low self-worth, lack of confidence and stress is a direct indication that truth is not operating in certain parts of your life. All of the above statements are bondage that causes the worst type of mental prison for the one who lives in it. The definition for the truth is that which is true; a statement or belief, which corresponds to the reality.

If the reality is twisted then so is your definition of truth.

ONLY TRUTH LIBERATES AND GIVES A BETTER QUALITY OF LIFE

And ye shall know the truth, and the truth shall make you free. John 8:32 (KJV)

I have discovered over the years that all of the people who I looked to for truth have not always had it even though they thought they had it. The very thought of inferiority to life's' challenges is a clear sign that truth is not operating in ones' life. The greatest point of truth that I have found is biblical truth. Bible truth sometimes goes against the wisdom of man and his perception of reality. The reason people are not successful is because they have not believed the Bible over circumstances, and words of others who were perhaps mentors. In every area of bondage in my life there is a truth given in the scriptures that will cause me to get untangled from it.

When the four words I-can't-do-this comes to your mind when you are working on your dreams you can combat that lie with God's word that says I can do all things through Christ, which gives me strength. Philippians 4:13 (KJV) The truth is given to make you free. Some people are so deep in mental bondage until at the very discovery of them seeing that this book is grounded in Bible truth is enough for them to put it down. But as the author of this work, I do not know of any other book than the Bible whose words have proven true throughout the test of time. So this will always be my foundation and pattern for true success, wealth, and happiness.

The many mental lies that you fight with has held your life back from the creators' ultimate plan of abundance for your life. Lies like you are not good enough or you are not smart enough, pretty, or handsome enough. You are too dumb or fat, skinny or black. It wasn't meant for you to be successful, powerful, and rich. All of these are lies that have held you back based upon something that someone or circumstances have placed into your belief system. Not one of the above statements is backed up and supported by the scriptures. There comes a point in our lives when we must agree with truth and reject every lie that comes to our minds.

We as a Christian nation have the most powerful gift at our disposal and many do not even know it or believe it. It's the book of all truths the Bible. We need to reprogram our minds.

Chapter 4

IT IS TIME TO REPROGRAM OUR COMPUTERS

If I am a know it all then I am stuck in my current position. Taking on a humble attitude and a teachable Spirit is the key to our success. First, there must be a separation from past knowledge and core beliefs that was based on lies and falsehood. We must admit to ourselves that there were some things from our past that we were taught that have never produced any good fruit in our lives. Yet we still practice those beliefs and not getting to our desired goal in life.

I often listen to people who argue about opinionated concepts and ideals that they think they can prove as fact. This proves that once a belief is instilled into the mind, whether it is wrong or it is right, it is always right to the one who believes it is right. But suppose those main beliefs that you hold so dear to your heart is a result of misinformed information. You will be surprised to know that after receiving truth and good direction how many people will not recant and back away from their old beliefs. The main reason for this type of attitude is pride. It does not take anything for someone to admit that there are others who know some things that you do not.

In order to re-program your mind you have also got to be willing to de-program it. You must be willing to do an honest analysis of what has already been input in your mind and separate the negative from the positive. Hold on to that which is beneficial, release, and let go of that which is not. It is a fact that the majority of the people in America have played so many different roles in trying to be accepted by others until they have lost their true selves in the process. The most important discovery that you can ever make is to rediscover self. Who are you really?

It is important that you learn to know and accept yourself even with your so-called imperfections. Today so many people have a self-hatred about

themselves and things that they do not have the power to change. I am too tall or too short or black or white. I am not handsome enough you know those same old self-inflicted lies. These are the lies that cause you to feel inferior about yourself and who you are. You cannot change those things about yourself so accept them and move on. However there are some things that you worry about that you can change. Things like your weight, financial situation, health, and happiness. The things that you can change about yourself (do not get frustrated with them) do something about it.

Every negative thing about yourself that you can change deletes it from your mental computer by working on it in order to change the results. Stop wasting time feeling sorry for yourself, get up, and do something about it. Only you can stop your progression. Everything that you perceive as being negative about you, that you cannot change maybe it would be a good idea for you to take a closer look at them. Some of the things that you may perceive as negative once you accept them can work out as hidden blessings. God did not make a mistake when he made you. So do not lie to yourself or let anyone else by telling you that there is something wrong with how God made you. God's word says that we are fearfully and wonderfully made. This means that no matter how you are made it is no mistake and God can and will get the best use out of your life if you will only let Him.

Letting God use your life means changing negative perceptions of self. This book is not a quick fix manual. The purpose of this book is to introduce and guide you into a new way of life of wholeness. It will help you to discover true success, which includes mental spiritual and financial prosperity.

IF LIFE WAS EASY WE ALL WOULD LIVE THE GOOD LIFE

The false concept of achieving your dreams of success without a struggle is very unrealistic. Once we understand, what is meant by the term what is worth having is worth fighting for. Then we can prepare ourselves for the battle that is ahead of us. Every child that comes through the womb of a woman is promised one thing upon entering this world, a struggle. Their first struggle is the one to get here. Once they get into this world, the struggle continues until the day they leave it. There is simply no such life on earth without problems and struggles.

Whenever we deceive ourselves into believing that life is easy then we become frustrated and feel like we are a target of bad fate. This is one of the reasons that people give up and quit on life. But the truth is that you really cannot quit life apart from suicide and even then, you will have to deal with the afterlife. You do not really have the option of quitting because either you will deal with life or life will deal with you. Either way you and life will meet, date and marry each other and depends on how you treat life will depend on how life treats you.

This shows that we are born with determination in us already. Have you ever stopped to think of how much determination it takes for a child to learn how to walk? No matter how many times that child falls down it just keeps on getting up and trying until they finally get it. There is just something inside of that toddler that will not allow it to quit until they have accomplished the goal of walking. If determination was not already in us from birth then we would not have learned to walk or even ride a bike. A lot of little children have more determination to overcome obstacles than adults. The reason for their determination is because they have not yet been taught to fail. Winning is natural but failure is a learned behavior. Based upon the environment that you were reared in determined the attitude that you have towards success or failure. Nobody was born to fail.

The reason that babies cry for what they want is because they honestly believe that they should have what they want. WOW now that is some powerful stuff. Do you honestly believe that you should have what you want out of life? Are you willing to take the necessary steps that it takes to get what you want? Those who will live the good life on earth are those who will choose to face every problem as a challenge that they must conquer.   Life's problems are like a puzzle. You have got to find the right pieces in order to make them fit. If you think on ways to overcome life's problems than your mind will give you the pieces that you need to solve life's puzzle.

People who are driven to succeed will always have problems. As a matter of fact, they will create their own problems in most cases. Problems cause us to think. They stretch and expand us when we solve them. For every problem that we solve it builds self-confidence and shows us that we are not limited in life. The more problems you solve the more you experience the invisibility of God in your life. Do not look at your problems as something that is put before you to destroy your dreams, but accept every problem as a challenge to move closer to your dreams being fulfilled.

The attitude that you should have towards your problems should not be dreadful but excitement! Life does not pose problems to you that you do not have the answer to. Any dream that you decide on seeing fulfilled in your life will invite problems with it. This is what I mean when I say that you create your own problems. The excitement comes when you realize that on the other side of the problem is the obtaining of the dream. Learn to attack your problem from every angle until you come up with the right solution. Refuse the very thought of ever giving up.

Stanley Arnold once said that every problem contains the seed of its own solution.

PROBLEMS AND STRUGGLES MAKE A STRONG BREED OF PEOPLE

"See, I have refined you, though not as silver; I have tested you in the furnace of affliction". Isaiah 48:10 (NIV)

Many of us wish for a world that was void of struggles and problems. We feel like if everything was good and there were no problems then there would be no worries and life would be just lovely. The only problem with that concept of life is we would never really learn what we were truly made of. Without problems, the world would remain stagnant and unproductive. Every single idea would go unchallenged because the success of ideas and dreams are birth through struggles.

Problems make the lives of people uncomfortable so that someone can challenge the discomfort and think of a way to restore comfort once again. In doing so, doors of growth, creativity, and invention are opened. God uses problems in order to bring about a change in the earth realm. Problems are not the result of some cruel fate.

Strong resistance and hardship always produce mental and spiritual growth. A man who knows how to endure problems will gain a greater insight of life after he come through one of life's storms. Problems should be accepted as a normal pattern for life. People who spend all of their time complaining about problems as if they are the only people who have them are not mentally healthy people.

Your success stories tend only to weaken the beliefs of others. Your problems and how you overcome them will impart strength to many. The conquering of your problems show that you are not the type of person who sits by and just lets life happen but you are willing to take charge of your life. You are always at your very best mentally in the midst of a storm. It is in the different times of life when the mind really starts to work on solutions. You do not learn much when things are going good but there is much to be learned in the struggles of life. Do not do your mind an injustice by lying down to a storm. Allow your mind to work even if it has to work overtime to bring about a new level of growth to your life. At the end of the storm, you will be more refined in life.

Chapter 5

YOUR GOD GIVEN ABILITY IS LEVERAGE TOWARD YOUR DREAMS

Then the disciples, everyman according to his ability, determined to send relief unto the brethren in Judea. Acts 12:29

Believe in your abilities. You cannot expect to achieve your dreams if you do not believe in yourself. Some people have discovered the thing about themselves that they do better than anybody else. Your God given ability is the answer to someone else's problems. You must learn to live and operate in the sphere of your own ability. Some people exercise their God given ability when it is convenient, but others constantly live a life style of utilizing their abilities.

It is important to know that God has not shortchanged anyone when it comes down to dispersing different gifts and abilities to mankind. In many of the Urban Cities of America, I have noticed that many of our youth are caught up in the drug trade. Before they started dealing drugs as a means of financial support, they did not believe that they had the ability to do anything. Some of these youngsters have organized drug enterprises that bring in more than a million dollars a year. The environment that they were reared in has molded and shaped their lives.

Many of these youth can be saved from a life of destruction if only they were taught to believe in their ability without limitations. The same way that they can organize drug empires is the same way that they can organize positive corporate businesses. The problem is they placed limits on their own abilities. I have heard many of them say "drug dealing is all that know." I want to encourage the readers to take the limits off of your abilities. Your ability is from God. It is a small piece to a gigantic puzzle and it is necessary that you display it before others in a positive manner.

Your ability will bring relief to someone else. It is a part of who you are. Whenever a person hides their abilities then they conceal the most beneficial

part of themselves to others. Your abilities can be used in a destructive or a constructive way it is all up to you. But the reason God gave you such a wonderful gift is so that you can make a difference in someone else's' life for the better.

Your abilities carry an awakening to a whole new way of life for someone else. For some people your abilities are like a breath of fresh air. The ability that you have is a gift from God to you, how you use it can be a gift from you to somebody else. If you use your ability in the wrong way, you may obtain wealth but you will never gain true happiness and satisfaction. It is only when you use your ability to bring relief and help others that you find life's greatest rewards.

Isn't that what life is all about being able to help someone else by doing that which comes natural to you? Accumulating money should not be your highest achievement but building a life with peace, love, joy, and wealth. Without peace, love and joy you will never enjoy wealth. In order to obtain you hopes and dreams you must develop self-confidence. By believing in yourself, you believe in the God that made you. There are so many people who are under achievers in life simply because they do not believe in their own abilities.

WEALTH IS CONNECTED TO YOUR ABILITY

"But remember the Lord your God, for it is he who gives you the ability to produce wealth …Deuteronomy 8:18 (NIV)

Although many people will not admit it in the church world, the truth is that God does not have a problem with His children having wealth. As a matter of fact, your wealth is locked up in your ability. The definition of the word wealth means an abundance of valuable material possessions or resources. Everybody has the ability to produce wealth. You must realize that everything that you will ever need to succeed in this lifetime is already inside of you. Granted, there is always room for us to improve on perfecting our abilities. But the truth of the matter is if we exercise them and believe in them then they will produce abundance and material possessions in our lives.

You will never express your abilities to the degree that it will draw wealth into your hands if you do not believe in its value. It is the people who know that they have something of value in their ability that is determined to keep promoting it until it yields the desired fruit of wealth. Everybody is born with hidden treasures of wealth already inside of themselves. The key is in learning how to market and promote your ability.

Most people spend more time thinking outwardly on situations and circumstances around them but they never look inside of themselves to discover their true self. An honest assessment of self will always open doors of self-awareness. To know one's self is the most important person that you can ever get to know. In order to discover your true self you must first start by separating with who you are not.

You are who you are when nobody else is around. The real you is not the actor and performer who you become when you are trying to impress

46

other people. I must submit that the real you is good. That

is the way that God the creator made you. The real you is uniquely different. The real you is special because of that reason. There are no two human beings that are exactly alike. Most people who are not comfortable in their own skin it is because they have never accepted all of their own uniqueness.

Today we live in a society that has set a standard for what type of person is accepted and what type is not accepted. The key way to rediscover yourself is by Prayer, Meditation and Deep heart searching. Stop looking outward for your identity and start looking inward. The person who has no regard for Spiritual insight will not benefit from this book. This book is full of Spiritual truth. I believe that if a person can master his or her spiritual life then they will master life period.

Prayer is getting self-discovery by the manufacturer who made you. The only one who can really give you some definition of self is God. Everyone needs to take at least one hour a day and ask God to show them themselves. After you finish praying, it is good to meditate and wait for the answer. God has put it naturally in the mind of man to discover answers to problems when they are diligently sought out. Mankind is nothing but a mind. We use every body part that God gave us in our daily lives.

As a matter of fact, we use some parts such as our arms, hands, and eyes more than other parts. But the most important part such as the mind we seldom use to its full potential. We rarely stretch our thinking capacity. It is so sad but for some people it seems as if it hurts them to think. I have watched people over the years that spend time to develop muscles on their bodies by lifting weights. Some even

develop strong cardio by running, hiking, swimming, biking etc.

This causing the heart to pump the blood throughout the entire body maximizing their circulatory health. Just as the physical body and the heart needs to be strengthened. Above all the main source of you (the mind) must be exercise by thinking. This is what meditation does. Prayer and meditation will begin to give you a vision for life that will become hard for difficult situations to refute. When you have discovered you then it makes it hard for anyone else to define you. That is what we call self-confidence. When you let, others define you that is lack of confidence.

Your abilities must be known and accepted by you. You must perfect them by believing

That nobody does it better or exactly the way you do it. In your times of prayer and meditation, start seeing yourself happy, successful, wealthy, and healthy. The mind will produce whatever it is that you can see and believe. Praying to God helps the mind to breakthrough self-imposed limitations. God has always used the mind as a place of invasion in order to impart His will, truths, and concepts. We must realize that the brain and the mind are two different things. The brain is the natural organ that controls the movement of every single part of the body.

But the mind is the Spirit of a person that controls the brain. The mind is Spiritual. Gods mind corresponds with your mind and He fills your with a positive view of yourself. Prayer automatically disposes of negative perceptions of oneself. You were made to achieve far more than most people ever will. Once you learn how to change your thought process about life then success will follow. I want to challenge you to stop living like a mistake and start living like an on purpose winner.

The reason I am stressing the point of knowing yourself is because a part of knowing self is knowing one's ability. Confusion of one's ability will always cause you to look at someone else's abilities. It is a waste of time for anyone to try to succeed at something that they are not gifted to do. Being honest with self will make you recognize that there are just something's that you cannot do and be successful at it. One of the biggest forms of deception is self-deception. Please remember that it is in the different things about you that no one does as well as you do. In the things that do easily is where you will find your wealth. It is important to know that God has placed His many treasures in our earthen vessels. One of those treasures is our abilities.

Chapter 6

PERSISTANCE PAYS OFF

"It is always too soon to quit." Norman Vincent Peale

Doctor Walker walked out of the dimly lit hospital room. From the looks of it folks, "I would say he has less than one month to live maybe sooner."

The cancer had spread throughout John Whitakers whole body. John Whitaker was a very cruel and obnoxious Oil Tycoon. Regardless of his massive wealth and fortune, it was not enough to cause his family to stick around. On this particular day, many of his family members had come to be at his bedside. Not because they cared for him but because they knew once, he was gone, someone would have to inherit his substantial wealth.

However, when all of his family had forsook him, his highly abused and under paid housekeeper, Pearl stuck by his side. After all, she often felt sorry for the grouchy old man. He prided himself on talking down to her. "You are the stupidest house keeper I have ever seen." He would often say. Whenever Pearl forgot to bring something as simple as cream for his coffee,

She would just smile and apologize. "I am sorry Mr. Whitaker. I should have paid more attention to what I was doing," She would often say. Throughout the fifteen years that she worked for him, she had often thought about quitting but something inside of her told her that if she continued to just hang on in there something good would happen for her one day. Every time the thought of quitting came up, she always managed to come up with a reason why she shouldn't quit. In other words, she self-motivated herself to continue on her course.

Johns' fate excited his family, however it saddened Pearl. The closer it got to the nearing of the thirty days Johns' family started planning how they were going to divide their inheritance among themselves. All of a sudden, a strange turn of fate happened. On day 27, John Whitaker sat up in his bed and started eating on an apple that was left on the nightstand. The nurse walked into the room and was astonished to witness what was soon to be a dead man sitting up so full of life. She was so surprised until she almost dropped the tray of medication she was holding. "Do not just stand there looking as if you have just seen a ghost, get moving and get me something to eat he said." The nurse quickly ran out of the door. "Doctor Walker it has got to be a miracle. I just do not understand what is going on." " Neither do I, said the good doctor."

The family heard the disappointing news of the sudden turn of fate. I cannot believe that God hates me that much that he would let that old buzzard live, said J. R. Johns' only son. J. R. quickly gathered up his family and boarded the next flight out of Dallas, Texas back to Lakeland Florida. One day while John was sitting alone in his hospital room in came Pearl. She walks in and does not say a word. She changes out Johns' water glasses; she waters the plants in his room, changes his bathrobe and props up his pillows. What are you still doing here aren't you going to leave like the rest of them John asked?

Don't be silly Mr. Whitaker nothing has changed this is what I do she said. Don't my constant nagging and dissatisfaction for the things that you do for me sometimes bother you? Haven't you thought about quitting this job and finding one that is easier? Yes, sir to be totally honest I have thought about it many times, but my father taught me years ago that quitting is not an option. The rewards always come to a person's life it they can only endure the difficult times in life. The problem with quitters is they go through hard times and give up. They never get to see the reward of what is on the end of their suffering.

John looked up at Pearl with tears in his eyes, "I am so sorry for any grief that I have ever caused you." "Please forgive me he said." I already have she responded. Pearl continued to clean and dust Johns' room when it comes a distinguished gentleman wearing a suit and tie looking very professional. "Could you excuse us for a minute Pearl? " John asked. Pearl quickly walked out of the room. One hour later the distinguished young gentleman walked out of the room and handed Pearl his business card. The card read Corey D. Mosley Attorney At Law. Mr. Whitaker said that you would need my card soon.

Pearl was perplexed "I do not understand why would I need and attorney" she asked? Pearl made an attempt to enter John's room but the young attorney stopped her. He is resting right now but he asked me to tell you to come back first thing in the morning. That night Pearl did not sleep a wink, she tossed and turned all night long. "What do I need a lawyer for; maybe he is firing me and wants to challenge me in court, she thought. One thought after the other tormented Pearl over and over again.

Finally, she dosed off to sleep and had a dream. She found herself in a field of dead flowers and off in the distance she saw a lot of run down houses. Then all of a sudden, children with sores on their necks and arms started coming out of the houses dressed in rags. The expression on their faces was one of confusion and want. At that, moment there was a deep desire in Pearl to want to help. She thought to herself what can I do? There was a plea of intense desperation to want to make a difference.

Then all of a sudden a voice from within said, "look behind the tree, retrieve the jug with the gold substance in it, and pour it on everything that you want to change." She first poured the gold substance

on the ground, the flowers began to bloom, and the grass of the fields began to turn green. Then she went up the hill and began to pour the substance on the steps of every house and they began to remodel themselves and they became brand new mansions standing firm and up right. The children walked up to Pearl with their mouths open, she began to pour the gold substance into their mouths, the sores began to clear up, and their garments changed into those of dashing splendor. Then the voice that was inside of her heart said, "The difference has always been inside of you."

Early the next morning Pearl mad her way to the hospital. Upon entering Johns' room, she came in contact with a nurse who was cleaning the linen off of Johns' bed.

The young lawyer was sitting silently over in a corner sorting through some papers. Where is Mr. Whitaker she asked? "He passed away in the night after he had me come in and change his will. It was almost as if he knew he was going to pass away during the night. He also left me this letter to give to you. Pearl reached out, slowly grabbed the letter from the Attorney, and immediately was gripped by its words.

"Dear Pearl, the difference in my life has always been in you. The unconditional love that you had for a grouchy old man like me and the uncanny ability that you possess to make others' lives better. Thank you for never quitting when quitting was not easy. To you I leave all of my wealth because I know that you will make someone else's life better even as you have mine."

Pearls persistence caused her to become a very wealthy woman.

The moral to the story is persistence always pays off and it is always too soon to quit.

Any dream that you would like to see come to pass in your life is going to take your persistence and a determined will not to give up. There is no such thing as the accomplishment of a dream without opposition. For every problem, that you face there is always a solution to it. Problems that we face do not give us an excuse to quit but it should motivate us to find a solution. The mind was given to us by God so that we can think. The mind is made for problem solving. Whatever your mind can conceive to believe you can achieve.

Jesus said it like this in Mark 9:23 "If thou canst believe, all things are possible to him that believeth."

Possibility thinking will always keep you moving forward toward your dream. (We will discuss Possibility thinking in more detail in a later chapter). Even when it seems as if you are not making progress forward, towards your goal by your staying on course, progress is still being made even if it is in your knowledge only. What we deem as opposition is really an opportunity for the mind to develop in the areas of creativity.

I would like to point out five primary reasons why quitting is not an option:

There is a reward for the one who does not quit.

Blessed is the man who perseveres under trial (opposition) for once he has been approved, he will receive the crown of life….James 1:12 (NASB)

There is always a reward in your continued persistence. Whenever you take on a new goal, challenge or dream opposition is promised to come.

We cannot allow ourselves to quit just because things do not go as smoothly as we think they should go. There is a great sense of accomplishment that you can enjoy when you know that the path that you traveled to achieve your dream was hard but you were one in a million who did not give up. We should not allow life to dictate to us what we are capable of but we should tell life what we will accomplish. The most powerful people in the world are those who have decided to take control of their own destiny.

<u>Knowledge of (HOW TO) is achieved when you do
no quit</u>

We have made mention that the mind of mankind is a master problem solver. When a person is consistent in achieving their goals and dreams, even when they do not know how they are going to accomplish the task, the mind will automatically begin to pull information from different directions in an attempt to find the answer to the problem at hand. Why do most people waste time taking on very small dreams? The truth is it takes just as much mind power (thought) to achieve something small as it does something great.

Decisions have been made all of your life in every moment of your life. Making decisions require thought. While trying to reach your dreams failure is necessary along the way. Nobody try's to achieve success and get it right at the first attempt. Failure causes us to weave through the things that are beneficial opposed to those that are not. It ultimately gives us the knowledge of how to achieve the dream.

The Inward Fight is Strengthened when a Person refuses to quit

Winners never quit and quitters never win!

You must come to a crossroad with yourself in life weather your comfort is important or the achievement of your dreams. If you expect everything to go your way without a fight then you are highly deceived on the concept of success. There are some people who can reach to achieve their goals in life as long as it is easy. But as soon as it gets hard for them, they quickly give up and look for a new goal that is easier. These types of people never accomplish anything.

They go through life jumping from one thing to another never to become successful at anything. By refusing to quit it causes you to become immune to obstacles that you will face along the journey to success. It also causes you to become strengthened within.

<u>When you refuse to quit it causes you to become unmoved by circumstances</u>

Now that you have learned how to persevere in the mist of opposition, the fear of failure is diminished. You will become unmoved in the face of adversity you have become a mountain mover, a giant slayer and like Christ our example a water walker. The main motivation for not quitting is prayer. Since man is Spirit, Soul and Body the person who builds up their Spiritual side will not be dominated by their natural circumstances.

<u>When you refuse to quit you experience growth</u>

We live in a world where stagnation is dominant among the people of this generation. Many of us have grown comfortable in living in the sphere of average. If we want to grow then we must be willing to experience growing pains of consistency. We expand to our fullest potential when we learn to meet our challenges head on. It is a wonderful feeling to walk and live on a plane that is above average. This level of growth is accomplished by refusing to quit whatever it is that you start.

Chapter 7

THERE IS NOTHING WRONG WITH YOU THEY JUST DO NOT UNDERSTAND

The difference in you is the best and real you. Those who will succeed are those who have discovered themselves, have accepted, and understand who God has made them to be. Many people are walking beneath their potential because they do not like the person in the mirror and so they try to be like someone who they admire. There is something terribly wrong with loving someone else, more than you love yourself. Jesus said in Matthew 19:19b that you shall love your neighbor the same way you love yourself. This means you can only love someone else to the degree that you love yourself.

Now when I am talking about loving yourself I am not talking about vanity, egotism, and pride. I am simply talking about one excepting themselves for what God has made them to be. Most people who avoid the concept of being a part of the masses can easily be perceived to be weird or strange. This is because the world that we live in has set a standard of what is normal and acceptable. This is why the majority of us never discover our own uniqueness.

People are literally afraid to be different. If you like, a lot of friends, acceptance and attention then you will never rise above what is expected of you by others. Becoming comfortable in your own skin is the best gift that you can give to yourself. If you are the type of person that constantly needs to be validated by, others, and then you are not in control of your fate, they are. Whenever you step out of the average pattern of what is perceived to be normal do not expect everybody else to blow horns and flutes in celebration on your behalf.

Negativity is a ruling force that governs the hearts of most people. You will also have to deal with jealousy and ignorance. If you are not selective about the people who you share your dreams with they will, out of ignorance, most times try to make you feel as if you are crazy for even having a dream.

ONLY A DREAMER CAN UNDERSTAND ANOTHER DREAMER

Maximizing potential, discovering purpose and achieving dreams is not a topic that everybody wants to discuss neither is it the desire of every heart. Walking alone is guaranteed when you are an achiever of success for a season. This is a part of the sacrifice that is mad for the sake of gaining wisdom, insight and understanding on how you are to make the dream become a reality. Do not expect others to understand you and your dreams. God gave you the dream so it is up to you to keep it alive. Others cannot kill it only you can abort it. This takes place in many different ways. Let us take a look at a few things that kill dreams.

THE NEGATIVE WORDS OF OTHERS ABORT THE DREAM IF YOU LISTEN TO THEM

Believe in your dream even if no one else does. It is yours God gave it to you and it is up to you to see it through. Do not expect others to see, feel, and believe in your dream. C-------- in the vision that God has given to you is an absolute must. The problem that most people face is they themselves have not allowed the dream to go beyond a good idea and a want. The key to accomplishing your dream must move you into the avenue of faith. There are many people who want to see their dreams come to past but they never see the reality of them.

Wanting to live your dream is not enough. Just be sure you get a good idea about something does not mean: 1. that it is your dream and two. That it is automatically going to come to past. I believe that your dream and your purpose cannot be separated and that they both come from God. Your dream should coincide with why your are. Finding that special place in life that you were born for is one of the most rewarding things that you could ever do by yourself. If your dream looks like something that you can easily accomplish then I seriously doubt that that dream is on that God gave you. Your dream from God will always be bigger than your human reasoning. You must dream big enough to put God in it. Refuse to live in the arena of normality.

You must find the reason for why you were created and walking, focus and live on that road. Believe it or not, every life has two roads by which it can travel. We like to call them the perfect will and the permissive will of God. On the permissive road, most people struggle with life although they may accomplish some great feats in life.

For instance, there are people who have gone off to school and have become what appears to most people as successful Doctors and Lawyers. But they were not happy even though they made a lot of money. But their dream was to be a professional musician. They can play music by ear on multiple instruments. They can write a song like other people write their names. Everything that has to do with music leads them directly into the perfect will of God for their lives. How does a person miss out on the perfect will of God?

Most of the time they let other people talk them out of pursuing their dreams. "Be realistic" they say, that is the craziest thing that I have ever heard! People will tell you, you are the wrong age, wrong color, wrong height, in the wrong frame of mind and the list goes on and on. If you listen to the negative words of others, they will kill your dreams. The dream is yours and just because others do not understand it, believe it, or like it, it is okay. They do not have to approve of your dream. As long as you keep your faith alive you will see your desires come to past.

Be selective about what you discuss with others. Be selective about your in crowd. You cannot discuss college curriculum with a fifth grade student. They are not qualified to communicate on that level of thought. College curriculum will totally overwhelm a fifth grader. The difference is they are on two different levels. Sometimes the road to greatness is a lonely journey. It is important for you to be confident enough to walk alone.

As time goes by life will put others into your life that think outside of the box. Eagles fly with Eagles. Great minds think alike. Surround yourself around unlimited thinkers. Get around people who believe in you and are confident in themselves as well. People are haters simply because of their lack of faith to believe that they can accomplish great things

 also. Whenever a person knows who he or she is and what their purpose in life is, he really does not have any room to hate on someone else.

Knowing your assignment and staying focused on bringing it to manifestation is a full time job. Come to the conclusion that a lot of people are just not on the same page as you are. You have made a decision that you are going to excel the average man or woman in life. So do not get upset just because other people may not be on your level.

MASTERING MY DREAM ZONE

Confidence, tenacity, faith, and refusing to quit even against the odds. You have got to find yourself in a mental zone that cannot be penetrated by the negative influence of others. Keep the dream ever before you by writing it out and making it visible so that you can meditate

On it. Have you ever seen Michael Jordan play basketball? I promise you it is an experience of a lifetime. The look in his eyes, the focus, and the concentration is so intense that it seems like in his mind that he is the only person on the court.

He literally does whatever it is that he wants to do even with nine other players on the court. In his own mind, he is living out his dream and he is in his zone. The crowd, the fans, the smell of hot dogs or anything else matters that is going on in the sports arena. It is show time and Mike has learned to Master his Zone. If a thousand people would have told him that, he could not play basketball it would not have mattered because he has tunnel vision. Find your zone and master it. Keep your dream alive by speaking it, walking it out, and writing it out.

TAKE OUT THE TRASH AND PUT IN A NEW LINING

Most people have been filled up with none beneficial thoughts. Those thoughts have molded and shaped our lives making them very unproductive. Thoughts of fear, failure, defeat, not being good enough, not being smart enough, handsome enough, pretty enough, inferior to other people, feeling as if others do not like you, you do not like yourself and the list goes on and on. These thoughts are trash that needs to be exposed of. It is time for us to take out the trash and put a new lining in.

In other words, those old thoughts must be replaces with new ones. Whatever is in the depths of a person's heart will form their belief system and a person's belief system will determine the quality of a person's life. So if I am going to change my life for the better I must deal with the issues of my own heart. Making positive confessions about one's self is a good way to start changing the condition of the heart. For every negative confession that I can capture I must verbally speak out the opposite. Positive thoughts and confessions about you is what I like to refer to as the thoughts and actions of God.

God does not want you to live and feel defeated in the only life that he has given to you. He wants you to make the most out of this life. Good wholesome and life changing thoughts must become a new way of life for you. Take the time out of you day to meditate and pray positive things over yourself. Visualize in your mind the quality of life you wish to have. Do not wait until you have every manifestation of what you are hoping and praying for, live as if you already visualized on the inside of you.

THERE IS JUST TOO MUCH STUFF IN THE GARAGE

There are people who do not throw away anything they try to save everything, even stuff they do not or cannot use. Before long, they have a whole lot of clutter lying around blocking the things that they really can and need to use. This is how some people's minds work. They have too many Irons in the fire. That means that they are trying to accomplish too many things at one time making your whole life unproductive. Singleness of thought and purpose helps one to stay focused.

Identify the thing that you want to accomplish and go after it whole-heartedly. If you are trying to do, a hundred things at once then get rid of some of those things and define what it

Is that you truly want to do. Every road that does not lead to your dream must be avoided. For some people it only takes what seems to be a better opportunity to present itself to cause them to get off course. In doing this, you are not taking charge of your destiny but you are taking what you can get. Some good ideas must be rejected and put on hold until your main objective is accomplished. You always want to maintain clear vision.

LET THE HARD TIMES AND OPPOSITIONS MAX OUT YOUR POTENTIAL

There is no such thing as accomplishing your dreams without opposition and difficulties. However hard times do not mean that it is an excuse for you to automatically quit and give up. There is a universal low that goes into effect when you become determined that you are going to accomplish the thing that you were born to do. Life doesn't automatically begin to expand you into the areas of growth that are needed. There is absolutely nothing that life brings to you as a challenge that you cannot handle.

The key to overcoming the challenges in knowing against what you can physically see. Your sight must be in your innermost being. You must learn to believe against circumstances and hope against what seems to be hopeless situations. You have to face difficulties as you would the Bully on the playground. "As a challenge" as it is with any fight, if you go into it feeling defeated then the outcome is not going to be good. But if you believe that you can win, and put up a good fight then the outcome is subject to be in your favor.

You must come to a place of understanding where you realize the opposition is presented to you by life to push you into greatness. There is a tremendous lesson to be learned through difficult times and if you persevere in the mist of it, all you will experience outstanding growth. For every attempt that you make to press toward your dream and you seem to fail, you learn how to go about it from a different angle until you finally figure it all out.

The potential inside of you is great and because of that reason, you have to be willing to be stretched in order to achieve greatness. There is nothing that life will present to you that you cannot face head on, that has been a problem for some people they do not face their problems head on. Instead, they run in the other

direction when trouble comes. You will never know what is fully on the inside of you unless you are willing to go through trying times with endurance.

You will discover that in time past you stopped running the race when in fact you still had enough wind left to keep on going. You can endure more than you think. So do not think. Just keep on pushing forward. Now do not misunderstand that last statement. Let me explain. Whenever negative reasons come to your mind, you cannot afford to think on them.

Chapter 8

ONLY ONE WAY TO TRUE HAPPINESS

Exterior or material things cannot make you happy. You have many people working two jobs trying to gather up enough stuff in hopes that they can find happiness in materialism.

Others move to beautiful geographical locations like the Caribbean Islands with its breath taking flowers and scenic Oceans hoping that the exteriors all around them will help them to find some kind of happiness. They always manage to come up short of their ongoing quest.

The fact has always been and it still remains that true happiness is an inward work of the Spirit and Soul of humanity. Man is a threefold being. He is a Spirit that has a Soul and lives in a Body. The fact is if the inside of a person is out of work then the whole life will be offset. If you are going to have the life that you have never had then you have got to be will to do what you have never done.

A bankrupt Spirit and Soul cannot give you a positive return in this life. You must learn how to build up your inward man (spirit). This is why Prayer and Communication with God is so important because prayer does for the Soul what food and nourishment does for the body. A person must understand that their true selves are more spiritual than physical and most of the time the Spiritual side of mankind goes unattended

FIVE STEPS TO HAPPINESS

Start your day with Prayer: As soon as your feet touch the floor, the very next stop that you should take is a moment of Prayer. While you pray allow God to minister to your heart about you day.

Take time out to read the Bible: The Bible is God's Word. The words from the Bible are Spiritual food and it is designed by God to connect with the human Spirit and bring Peace, Joy, Strength and Hope into the life of the reader.

Meditate on what you have read: Allow the Word of God that you read to soak into you like a sponge by meditating on what you have reader.

Sow goodness and kindness into other people's lives: Making the quality of others' lives better helps your life to become filled with Joy. The scriptures say we reap what we sow, what you do for others God will do for you.

Ask God in Prayer for your purpose and walk in it: True happiness is found in the reason for why you were created.

True happiness is always a condition of the heart. It is never found in an exterior or any material items but it is a need for an inside job. When I mention the heart, I am not talking about the organ in the center of your chest that pumps blood through your body. I am talking about the core of who you are. I am talking about the very soul of who you are.

Candy, Soda Pop, Cake and Cookies is so good to the taste but it is deadly to the body if too much is consumed over a period of time. This is the same thing with your Spiritual life, which produces true happiness. You must develop a healthy spiritual diet. Learn to feed on the good vegetables of Prayer, Bible scriptures, Meditation on God's Word, Sowing good things into other people's lives, and walking into your God given purpose.

There is a truth that is rarely exposed to mankind when it comes down to being happy. There are so many ways that people go about trying to find happiness is a Spiritual problem. You cannot be happy without the development of the inward man. Look on the inside and do an honest assessment of yourself and be willing to empty out those things that are not causing you to progress toward happiness. Start Today!!! Make a conscious decision to be happy and go for it.

Chapter 9

LIFE CHANGE IS UNCOMFORTABLE

Whenever a person decides that, they are going to change their lives for the better it is necessary for them to become uncomfortable in the process of change. Change means doing things differently from the way you were used to doing them. Changing the mind alone does not bring about change but changing the actions as well. There are people who think on doing things differently everyday but the problem is they never put action to their thoughts.

If you are used to living in the Sphere of average, then breaking away from that cycle can become very uncomfortable. Once you have been used to doing something a certain way then those ways are not easily broken. The old way of doing things really was not leading you in your full potential but at least you kind of had the old pattern figured out. But the new way of living is leading you to the fulfillment of your dreams but it is almost like walking through life with a blindfold on. You must realize that you will never get different results by following the same old pattern.

Change takes boldness and courage. Walking in courage will put you in a lot of uncomfortable places. This is one of the reasons that most people live their lives by only Inspiring to get a good job, a family a car and a house with a white picket fence. This is what we call living the average American dream. Most people work all of their lives to achieve these few simple things in life. But the dream can be much, much bigger if you are willing to get out of your comfort zone and do things that you are not used to doing.

The feeling of awkwardness only means that change is taking place. People who love comfort will not experience high levels of success. Successful people are those who have learned to live a life a part

from their comfort zones. A lot of these principles that I am writing in this book demand the reader to do some things that they have never done but if they are followed then they will produce the life that they want and deserve. The things that you are doing in life have gotten you to where you are now. If you are not living your dream then this means that there is room for alterations in your life.

Most of the things that make you uncomfortable are things that you really need. In order to make a difference in this world then I have got to be will to be uncomfortable. One of the things that I do in life is minister the Word of God. That is my purpose, but before discovering my purpose, public speaking was totally out of the question. I just did not have an outgoing personality. The first time I had to speak to a congregation of people, I was very uncomfortable.

In spite of my nervousness and insecurity, I mustered up some courage and a whole lot of boldness. For me speaking in public was very uncomfortable but after doing it over and over, it became natural. Now the greatest fulfillment in my life is when I minister the Word of God.

Before most people move out to fulfill their dreams everything has to be all nice and comfortable. This is exactly another reason why people do not live their dreams. Now I am not saying that we should not minimize the struggle that is up ahead by carefully planning. But what I am saying is that even after you plan you have got to take a risk. Taking a risk is not always comfortable but it is something that you must do if you are going to live out your dreams.

One of the things that I have discovered that helps me to break out of my comfort zone is in doing things that go against comfort like working out with weights, running and exercises like push-ups, squats and jumping jacks. These things bring a lot of discomfort to the body but they are good for me. A lot of uncomfortable situations are really good for us. In working out, I purposefully put myself in these uncomfortable situations expecting the end results will be to my best benefit.

There are many men and women who have been divorced and have lost everything. They have lost wife, husband, some have lost children, homes, cars and everything. They are now stuck because they now realize that there is nothing left. All of the accomplishments that they have achieved with their former spouses are now gone. And God forbid that they are now up in age 40 years plus. This puts you in a very uncomfortable situation to perform in life and move ahead.

You have built already and thinking back on the time and effort that it took you to accomplish the life that you had it seems as if a whole lot of work was put in. Now it is time to live the real life that you were supposed to have in the first place. Allow the excitement of walking onto a new path to overwhelm you. You now have to refocus and understand that if you could not handle the lost then you never would have lost because life does not hand you things that you cannot handle. Take those lemons and turn them into lemon aid.

Do not let people take you, rape you, and stop you by their decisions towards you. When it comes, down to rebuilding your life it becomes very uncomfortable but do it any way. There is a beautiful life after divorce. Now you can focus on yourself and become whole. There are so many people who have laid down in life because of losses that took place in their lives and they did not know how to handle them.

So they just threw in the towel and gave up the fight in life.

Whenever we embrace the attitude of being uncomfortable, that is when we find ourselves in uncomfortable situations that were forced upon us by life we do not quit but we continue to move on. Life itself will force you into uncomfortable situations that you yourself had no power over by causing crisis situations to occur. Things like divorce, death, loss of job, friends, finances etc. All of these things can be snatched away from you at any moment thus making you very uncomfortable. This is life's growth process; this means that it is now time for you to grow up.

THE STORY OF THE EAGLE

Whenever the eagle is born, the mother makes the nest very comfortable and cozy.

She brings the hatchling everything that it needs to snuggle up in comfort. She spreads her wings out over her Eaglets to protect them from the storms and the rain so that they can stay warm and dry. She brings them their food on a daily basis. But this comfort does not last. There comes a day when the Mother knows that her baby eagles must get out of the nest and SOAR on their own. That is when she purposely makes the nest very uncomfortable.

The mother eagle fly's out of the nest and she gathers thorns a little at a time and one day at a time and puts them in her nest making it very uncomfortable. Every move that the little eagles make they are pricked by thorns which causes them to desire to get themselves into a new position but it does no good because before long that whole nest is full of thorns.

Finally, the little eagles cannot take it anymore and they jump out, soar, and never look back.

They move out to discover a new life. Let your uncomfortable situations cause you to take a leap of faith into a New Life. I know that sometimes life is painful but take your pain and let it push you into progress. The uncomfortable process is a must if you are ever going to fly with the eagles.

We must recognize the thorns of life as our help; they are supposed to push us into a new level of life, growth, and development. When a person is uncomfortable, it is life's warning signs that something is about to or should change in your life. It is okay to be uncomfortable especially when you have goals ahead of you that require you to get out of your comfort zone.

the key in handling uncomfortable situations is by waiting it out and pushing forward until it becomes normal to you.

Chapter 10

BECOMING FEARLESS

We all have heard acronym of the word FEAR. False Evidence Appearing Real

When it comes to achieving your dreams in life, you have got to be willing to do whatever moral things possible that will cause your dreams to become a reality. The road to success demands that you take a lot of unfamiliar paths and this alone can be scary. You will be faced with many squeaks and bumps in the dark meaning many mental spooks.

Do you remember when you were a child how you felt about going to bed after staying up and watching a horror movie? Whatever you saw in that movie that night in your mind, it was either in your closet or under your bed. Throughout your course of life, you have watched the big screen of your _____. You have witnessed the many successes and failures of those around you. Somehow, the failures are what stood out the most in your mind causing unrealistic expectations.

This is how fear confines us and binds us. You will never be the best you that you can be by allowing fear to dominate your life. When it comes down to facing your fears then you must develop a Star Trek mentality. Do you remember the Star Trek gate? Let me reiterate. These are the Voyagers of the Star Trek Enterprise. Their mission is to seek out New Life and New Civilization. To boldly go where no man has gone before! In order for us to face new challenges and ventures then we must muster up boldness. You will never go anywhere in life without the boldness to face your fears.

Boldness is not the absence of fear but it is the courage to face them anyhow. Lack of boldness has allowed fear to keep people so confined and incarcerated in the prison of circumstances until they never seem to have the nerve to progress. What a terrible predicament for anybody to find themselves in. The truth is that this is the place where most people live. God our creator desires that we should never be hindered by fear. He wants us to learn these principles that lead to fearlessness.

The truth is that most of your fears are false alarms, most of your fears are the monsters in the closets, and under the beds that you faces when you were a child. Most of the fears that torment and bind you are not real. In the Bible God told his servant Joshua over and over to take courage. He told Joshua if he took courage and followed his instructions that he would experience great success. But he also told Joshua that Joshua's own doings would cause him to experience prosperity.

The overall goal was to cause Joshua to go in and possess a land that God had promised to a whole generation. But God needed someone who had courage and were not easily overwhelmed by the negative things that would face them. He was letting him know that based upon the relationship that Joshua had with him he did not have a need to worry about what he would face on the road that he had ahead of him.

In order to accomplish the purpose and dreams that God intended for your life you have got to take courage. It takes courage to walk in faith and not see the manifestation of the dream that is only in your head. You will be faced with a lot of thoughts that will tell you why you will never be able to accomplish the dream. These negative thoughts must be pushed out of your mind and you must take a chance anyway. Building and developing a trusting relationship with God will always give you the ability to conquer your fears. The roof of fear is a depraved Spiritual Life.

God never comes in contact with His people without giving them a better quality of life. When we realize this important fact then it automatically should impact a sense of courage in us. Lack of true success (and notice the word T-R-U-E) is because of lack of relationship with God. The definition of true success that I am talking about is wholeness of mind, body, and finances. So many people have one or the other but not all three areas are completed in their life.

God wants us to have life and have it more abundantly. It was in the plan of God for us to live and not only exist. God wants us to enjoy our lives. Fear draws negative things into our life. It is a tool of Satan that he uses to get open doors into your life. If you fear a thing long, enough then it will manifest and become a reality. Fear is not a seed that we can allow to grow in our lives. When we recognize that we fear something then we must quickly confront it and throw out the thought. Fear of danger, death, failure, success, and the many others that come into our lives are not worth the attention that most people give to them.

These things when feared have a tremendous paralyzing force behind the thought. Let us see what the Bible has to say about fear drawing unfortunate things into our lives.

"For the thing which I greatly feared is come upon me, and that which I was afraid of is come unto me". Job 3:25 (KJV)

Can you see from the scripture in Job how the thing that was constantly tormenting his mind finally visited his life? Job walked around for only God knows how many years in a constant state of fear.

If you know the story of Job, then you know that he lost his property, family and finally his health. This was his statement that came forth out of his mouth because he harbored the fear of losing all in his heart. He admitted that the thing he was afraid of had found an opportunity to creep into his life and bring his fears into reality. This was the reason the devil knew what to ask God for permission to attack him with. The Bible lets us know that Job honored and respected God but he did not really trust in God.

Too many of us are too connected to the affairs and cares of this world. This is why we must talk with a Spiritual mind set. The Spiritual mind decides that it is good to trust God. There is no fear in trusting in God because He is bigger than all of our fears. This alone should comfort you in every fear that will come up against you. We cannot afford to look at what the situation appears to be but we must look past it into the deliverance of God. Fear binds you but God wants to deliver you. If you want to get over fear there are some things that you have got to do that goes against the nature of our fears.

THERE ARE SIX WAYS TO COMBAT YOUR FEARS

Understand that most of the fears that you face are not real. Most of these fears come to rob you out of the quality of life that God wants you to enjoy.

Pray and ask God for boldness to press forward even when there is fear or apprehension about your situation, move, or endeavor. This is called courage.

Realize that the only real failure is the one who fails to try. Do not let fear stop you from trying.

You must understand that fear is not something that we must have in our lives. It is a choice to accept or reject your fears.

You must realize that when you face your fears and go against them anyway then you develop power over them, but when you refuse to deal with them then they can literally destroy you.

You must realize that fear is satanic and not of God. The Bible says that God does not bring torment into our lives. If we are tormented by anything then we must understand that it is not of God. "For God hath not given us the Spirit of fear, but of Power, and of Love, and of Sound Mind. Two Timothy 1:7 (KJV)

CHAPTER 11

YOU ARE NOT A MISTAKE BUT A PURPOSE

The reason that you were ever born is because there was an empty purpose and plan that needed the right body, mind, and personality in order to fill it. You were created for a purpose. I cannot stress this point enough. Then you may ask the question why is mankind so misplaced in this world? That is because people are trying to find their place from their own intellect.

I would like to say that you will never find out who you are or why you are by trying to figure it out. The maker of a product is the only person who really knows all of the ingredients that are in side of it. In order for us to understand the potential plan and purpose of our lives, we must go back to the maker, who is God. He knows everything that He has placed in side of us, He alone can define us. Before you were ever born you were a thought of affection in the loving and caring mind of God. Today you have people dying and running around aimlessly trying to figure out all of life's problems when in reality they just really need to let God first show them themselves and how they fit into the whole scheme of things.

Let us see what the Bible has to say about you being a purpose to the world.

Jeremiah 1:5 says, "Before I formed thee in the belly I knew thee; and before thou comest forth out of the womb I sanctified thee, and I ordained thee a prophet unto the nations."

Before Jeremiah was formed in his mother's belly, he was in the mind of God. God is the only

one who really knew you? Have you ever heard people say, "I do not even know myself?" Well this saying is truer than naught. It is good for a person to

112

separate himself or herself in prayer and ask God to show them who they really are.

The detriments of low self-esteem and insecurities have caused many to live on a defeated level in life. If a person could consciously capture every defeating thought that runs rampant in their minds then they would be able to go against them. The problem is some of those unhealthy thoughts catch us by surprise. They have been so much a part of you makeup until it makes you very uncomfortable to come up against them.

What is the voice that is in the atmosphere that is stealing mans' self-worth and over all identity? There is an enemy that attacks the mind and situations of mankind. His goal is to lose you in is agenda. His agenda is totally negative for your life. Sometimes he will put abundant finances in the hands of those with a darkened soul. This helps them to continue to destroy themselves and keep them misplaced even longer. John 10:10 clearly speaks of this unseen enemy that attacks our purpose and destroys it. "The thief cometh not, but for to steal, and to kill, and to destroy: If I can convey one message from this book and that would be, "Stop letting the devil steal from you!" You have to put your foot down and say enough is enough. Do you realize that you do not just have a purpose but you are a purpose?

You are the answer to someone's problem, the piece to someone's' puzzle and you are not just called to make a difference in this world that we live in. When we look across America, we can easily see the detriment of a mis-placed Generation and its effects. There is no heart in them to know their purpose. Most of them have bought into the lies that they are worthless, not important and an under achiever. There is no hope in the world except through Jesus Christ.

If you want, a fulfilled and full life there is no other way. The second part of John 10:10 says..."I came that they might have life and might have it super abundantly". It is Jesus who wants to give you the greatest quality of life. The more you discover your why in life is what I am promoting throughout every page in this book. The overall truth is there is no such thing as a life without disappointments, trials, and struggles but at the end of the day there is a peace that passes the human intellect.

As you go through life it is important for you to know that you are not a mistake, do not believe the deceptive thoughts that bombard you mind. The discovery for what you were created for is found in your commitment and surrendered relationship with Jesus Christ. This May sound simple but it is the only truth.

EVERY TRUE PURPOSE IS ESTABLISHED BY THE HOLY SPIRIT

Every purpose is established by <u>counsel</u>: and with good advice make war. Proverbs 20:18 (KJV)

And the Spirit of the Lord shall rest upon him, the spirit of wisdom and understanding, the spirit of counsel and might...Isaiah 11:2a (KJV)

In Isaiah, the Bible speaks of the Spirit of Counsel. The spirit of counsel is also known as the Holy Spirit. In Proverbs, it speaks about every purpose being established by counsel. What better counsel can one receive as far as purpose is concerned that from the one who mad you that is the Holy Spirit. Outside of God, most people believe that they are living but in all actuality, they merely exist. Being able to take consistent counsel from the Holy Spirit will bring you into that place that is fulfilling to the heart. By being in tune with the Holy Spirit He will lead you right smack dab into your purpose.

Counsel of the Holy Spirit is not something that you can hear with the natural ear but with the heart. Becoming sensitive to the Spirit is cultivated by developing an ongoing prayer life. Day by day as you walk with God in prayer, the divine direction of the Father will land you into your purpose. If at all possible, before you go to God in prayer let your mind be set at ease. Be open to listen for the inward promptings of your heart.

You must understand that there is a divine mandate that is upon your life and it is only understood by your connecting with God's Spirit through prayer. Mind Idolatry is when you think that all of the understanding and guidance that you that you will ever need is derived by

Your ability to think study and learn. It is when you have made up your mind your greatest point of

117

information. It is when a person begins to look inward

instead of outward for assistance. There is something that is called revelation knowledge and it does not come from within but it comes by looking to the Spirit of God. It is when He unveils hidden truth and opens you up to a new thought process.

There has always been a hidden unseen force that has had influence on the thoughts of mankind. The very thoughts of those who have committed their lives totally over to God will be able to recognize where each influence is coming from. The Holy Spirit will move up on your heart regarding your purpose.

I Corinthians 2:9-10 says "But as it is written, Eye hath not seen, nor ear heard, neither have entered into the heart of man, the things which God hath prepared for them that love him. But (He) God hath revealed them unto us by his Spirit: for the Spirit searcheth all things, yea, the deep things of God." (KJV)

Notice the mentioned verse says God has prepared some things for us that we have never seen and heard before. This refers to those who do not have a clue about their purpose. The Bible lets us know that some of the things that God wants to give us is not something that we have been taught or studied. Because through studying and teachings you can enter things into your own heart. But God tells us that some of the things that he has prepared have not been processed through the heart.

It is not the will of God for us to live a life of low living. Our perception of God has been flawed by the dictates of this world. There are those who do not believe that God wants anything good for them to enjoy while they are on the earth. That frame of mind could not be further from the truth. The very desire to search for truth and meaning to this life has been stolen from countless people. And some people get it all mixed up by believing that because a person has a

talent that has brought them fame and money that they must have discovered their purpose. But there can be nothing that deceives people like false purpose.

The way that you know when you are living out a false purpose is lack of fulfillment. When purpose is discovered and established there is satisfaction and peace. As a matter of fact I dare to say that the most fulfilled you will ever be is when you discover your purpose.

EVEN JESUS WAS GIVEN A DISTINCT PURPOSE BY GOD THE FATHER

…."For this purpose the Son of God was manifested, that he might destroy the works of the devil." I John 3:8b (KJV)

When Adam and Eve sinned in the Garden of Eden, it was the result of a master plan that Satan had conjured up in order to gain control over everything that God had rightfully given into the hands of men. At one point, the fellowship between God and mankind was so close until there was simply no mistaking in his hearing the voice of God.

The Bible says that Adam walked with God in the cool of the day. Now Satan being an enemy of God he decided that since he could not defeat him that he would touch and destroy that which is close to his heart and he would corrupt and contaminate mankind. The feud started when an act of rebellion on Satan's part took place in heaven. God created Satan for the purpose of bringing in the worship of heaven. He was known as the Anointed Cherub. This Angel was one of the most beautiful and gifted angels in heaven. Even though he had a purpose of the highest honor this old winged creature was not content with what God had given him he wanted what God had. That was the worship that only belongs to the creator of everything.

Somehow the Bible does not say how exactly Lucifer (Satan's name at the time) took one third of the heavenly host of Angels and led them into a rebellion against God in an attempt to take over the abode of God. And the Bible says that by the finger of God Satan and those who he led into that act of rebellion was thrown down to the earth. It makes you wonder if God is using Satan to bring His greatest creation into God's plan and purpose. Just think about it out of all the places where God could have cast Satan too, why did he send him to the earth?

Did He not know that shortly thereafter He would create man and please him in that same earth?

This is where we pick up on the Adam and Eve story.

By causing them to sin by eating the forbidden fruit Satan gained access to their minds, giving those desires that would impart the very nature of Satan himself. Selfishness and Pride were now evident in the hearts of mankind. The desire to want to rebel against God was now adopted.

Mankind became a deprived and rebellious people. The work of Satan was now complete. His oppressive power now dominated the lives of men and women. Adams sin opened up the door and the Devil barged right on in to e_____ his intended plan. Remember the worship that he wanted now through the false god system of Babylon that worships became a reality. It was that same rebellious nature that Satan had imparted into Adam and Eve it went on to transfer through the bloodline to affect everyone who comes from his seed which just so happens to be the entire human race. Mankind wanted something more than God. They wanted to make their own forms of God that would cater to the nature and desires of the one who had deceived them.

They created gods that would allow them to appease their sensual appetites over riding their own conscious and any rational and moral thinking of the true and living God. The brutal effects of the work of the wicked and cruel adversary. What was to be done about such a heinous offense? It is important to know that the very purpose of why mankind was created was lost by the demonic encounter with the devil. The life of mankind became bent, twisted, and perverted. The abnormal had become the normal.

The vicious sting of death had entered the world. Death by separation from God, death of purpose,

123

awareness of self and ultimately death that resulted in the grave. God had to legally bring back his creation into the life that he intended for them to have. After

all so very much was lost during man's fall. How would mankind recover everything that mankind forfeited to the enemy? There was only one way. God the Father looked over at Jesus His Son and the Son said I already know the purpose. Now prepare for me a body.

Then according to Galatians 4:4 when the fullness of time had come, God sent his Son born of a woman, who was made under the law. The word fullness in the Greek is PLEROMA and it means to supplement or to fill the space that empty. In other words in the times of emptiness and times when it seems like something was just missing God sent a method of completeness into the times. Jesus came into the times in order to bring completion to every void in life. This is still the purpose of Christ that He may fix every broken life that the devil has tried to destroy. The devil through Adams disobedience left a pattern of destructive works. But Jesus came for the purpose to clean up the destruction that has plagued mankind from the beginning of time. In Jesus every demonic work is destroyed, even blindness to your purpose.

Now do you remember that I said I wondered if God is using Satan in order to push mankind into Gods plan and purpose? As a matter of fact, that is exactly what God is doing. Satan is the pressure that drives men right smack dab into the purposes of God. Everything under heaven has a purpose even our enemy. Satan is too stupid to realize that by him wearing mankind down and causing them to feel trapped like a mouse caught in a rattrap.

What he is really doing is causing people to do is look for answers of relief. In doing this, men and women are coming out from under his regiment. To put it a better way mankind runs to God and then He finds help but not only that but a sense of purpose. Now this

purpose must be sought in prayer. Jesus came to fine-tune your life by destroying every single work of the devil in your life.

The Father's triumph is when He died on the cross and every single thing that concerns

 you living at a higher quality of life was taken care of. This is the reason He said IT IS FINISHED.

To farther prove my point let us take a look at what John 10:10 says again. The thief comes not, but for to steal and to kill, and to destroy: I am come that they might have life, and that they might have it more abundantly.

Here Jesus explains two different purposes from two totally opposite spiritual sources. Each has a purpose but the one that has the only beneficial benefits is Jesus. Jesus is not satisfied with you just existing but He wants you to live on the abundant level. Other Greek words for abundantly is a life of Preeminence and Super Abundant that gives you and advantage.

The sole purpose of this book is to strategically take back through the wisdom of Jesus everything that the devil has stolen from you. The birds, bees, trees, sun, air, and the clouds, everything in this earth serves a purpose for something or someone else and so do you. Everybody has been given a limited amount of time in the earth and during the time that we have been given, we must discover our place. In doing this we add a beneficial quality to the world.

Even as Jesus completed an empty place in the world, so do you. This makes you think on the broadness of life and this is only a thought of how far society and the world would be if we all walked in our purpose. It is sad to say but many people will go

through this life struggling and lost with no different aim. Life for them will become a task and a tedious routine. You do not want to end up like that!

For you who hold this book and apply its knowledge in your life you will excel and enjoy every day that you are alive. The things that I have written to you are not something that is beyond your grasp or comprehension. These are just simple oversights that must people tend to overlook. Remember that before you were brought forth into this world your design and purpose was already thought out by God himself. With the creation of you there was no mistakes allowed.

POSSIBILITY THINKING

Jesus said unto him, if thou canst believe all things are possible to him that believeth. Mark 9:23

In chapter 6, we briefly wrote on the topic of possibility thinking. I thought that it was so vital that we discuss this topic in detail until I know that I had to dedicate an entire chapter to it. Possibility thinking is the ability to think without limitations. If you look at any particular task in life as impossible then you are reading the right book. I want to start dealing with your core belief system. Because what you truly believe, about whom you are and what you are capable of what you deserve and what you are willing to sacrifice to have it all deals with your belief system.

I call it a belief system because it is a system of thought based up on how your mind was programmed by your upbringing. There were things and events that took place in your life at a very early age that dictated to you how high your world rises in life or if you were capable of achieving things that would impact a nation, generation and even the world. The expansion of a dream always starts in the mind.

Those walls of (can't) have been erected and they are massive and even intimidating but they can and will be brought down. The reason children have such strong imaginations is because they do not have the limited thinking ability that most adults have. Believe it or not, you were taught to think in the sphere of limitations. Most of those limitations were placed on you by Parents, Teachers, Preachers, Peers and others whose opinion you valued. Those people meant well when they said things like "think realistically, that is not logical you need to stop doing all of that stupid dreaming. No that can never happen." They unknowingly programmed you to think on what society considers being normal.

You were reared and raised by the level of someone else's' belief system. Since they did not believer that they could achieve big things in life they called themselves protecting you by opening up your eyes to common sense. But who wants to be common, common only means normal or average. But whenever a person lives in the realm of the impossible then they will exceed the common. Now do not get me wrong we should think things through in order to come to a reasonable decision.

At the same time, we must not allow human reasoning to predict to us what we can and cannot accomplish. All the power that has flowed through your life that allowed you to accomplish the things that you have already done is a result of your belief system. Whether your accomplishments were large or small possibility, thinking allows you to enlarge your sphere of thought that you in turn will get giant results. And remember everything is small to a giant.

When the thought comes to your mind to achieve something the following thought should be "I can." Notice that the above scripture says that all things are possible if you can believe. As a matter of fact, Jesus is the one who said it. Negative beliefs about other people, yourself, your abilities, about God, about your children, your parents, success, failure and life as well as other things have been a stronghold in the lives of so many people. Those beliefs have walked you into your own mental world.

However, there is that something deep down on the inside that is longing to be free. Those core negative beliefs have to be replaced by positive thoughts. There must be a point in your life where you have discovered that your life is not moving forward. The question you have asked your self is what is wrong? There is an agitated and somewhat a grieved feeling

that comes upon us whenever we partake in any negative activity. There is just that eerie feeling that we get in the pit of our stomachs. This is the belief system that must be torn down.

Notice it says all things are possible to him that believes. You can believe either negative or positive but whatever way you believe you bring the possibility of it into your life. This is why the devil works overtime bringing negative thoughts to your mind because he knows that if he gets enough of them into your belief system then they will determine the outcome of your life.

POSSIBILITY THINKERS TRUST GOD

"And Jesus looking upon them saith, With men it is impossible, but not with God: for with God all things are possible. Mark 10:27 (KJV)

Self-reliance is not the thing that I am trying to promote. But I am esteeming the power that goes beyond the human abilities. The entire process of change that I am talking about will have everything to do with a change of Spirit that produces a change of thoughts, which will produce a change of life style.

Possibility thinking must first start within your heart. It takes a sincere relationship with God in order for you to go beyond what seems to be impossible with men. Most great feats are

Accomplished by way of hidden spirits working with human agencies. I realize that this is a bold statement but let me explain there is only two agendas of thought in the earth realm. One that promotes God's causes and the other that promotes Satan's' causes. Spirits are unseen forces with personalities that speak, hear, and express themselves through human beings. These spirits are known throughout the Bible as demons. They have been known to give mankind a sense of success but it never satisfies.

On the other hand, the Bible says that God is a Spirit and He sends to man His Holy Spirit. God's spirit also moves upon the mind of man and influences his thoughts and abilities for the good of mankind. The good news is Gods Spirit has no limitations and when his Spirit connects with the Human spirit, you do not have any limitations either. This makes you a supernatural person. This means God takes His super ability and connects it with your natural.

In trusting ourselves to God, we develop the mind and insight of Christ. If you know anything

about Him then you know that He went around defying natural universal laws. He never took on the mind set of limitations and for every problem He brought the solution.

"For who hath known the mind of Lord, that he may instruct him? But we have the mind of Christ." I Corinthians 2:16 (KJV)

When we think through the mind of Christ, we began to break through barriers of resistances. We become unconfined, unhindered, and unrestricted in our thinking.

What is it that has haunted you throughout your life that you would really like to see become a reality? Do you not know that those thoughts and ideas could very well be the desire of God for you also? But the thought of how inferior you are to the dream of you heart has caused you to believe in your heart that you cannot accomplish what you truly desire. This is the only reason that people settle for second best. There comes a time when you have just got to trust God and go for it. Every real believer has access to the Mind of Christ. Christ never faced anything that He thought was impossible to deal with to conquer or to do.

POSSIBILITY THINKING SEES THE REWARD FIRST THEN GOES BACK TO FIGHT OFF THE HINDERANCES

And they came unto the brook of Eshcol, and cut down from thence a branch with one cluster of grapes, and they bare it between two upon a staff; and they brought of the pomegranates, and of the figs. The place was called the brook Eshcol, because of the cluster of grapes, which the children of Israel cut down from thence. And Caleb stilled the people before Moses, and said, Let us go up at once, and possess it; for we are well able to overcome it. Numbers 13:23, 24, & 30 (KJV)

In the above scriptures is the primary thought process of a possibility thinker vs. an impossibility thinker. The children of Israel went into the land that God had promised them and they saw how rewarding the Land was. They even admitted that the land was pleasant and it flowed with milk and honey. But in their eyes, it looked impossible for them to inhabit it based on the natural situations and circumstances. Their own fears had them paralyzed from moving forward into the perfect desire of God that He wanted for them.

The move that God had orchestrated for them was truly a good move but they were not at the spiritual or mental level to receive the blessing that God was trying so desperately to give them. The idea of fighting for what they wanted was totally out of the question. I want you to understand these were Gods chosen people and He had personally intervened in their lives over and over again but somehow they still were not able to believe Him for a victory over the enemies that stood in the way of the promises He had given them.

They saw the task of conquering the land as impossible; they saw the people as being stronger than themselves but forgot that the God that they served was all-powerful. They saw the Giants also known as the Son of A-Nak but failed to realize that God was even bigger. They saw that the cities were walked in but they should have seen that God had the power to tear down the walls. All they could see was the problems but not the solution to the problem.

Why do you suppose that these people who belong to God felt so powerless in retrospect to achieving the thinking that God wanted them to do? The difference was in relationship with God. There was one of them whose name was Caleb. When all of the others were talking about what they could not do; Caleb had a strong personal relationship with God he knew that he could not fail. He did not only believe that he was able to inherit the promise of God he knew he was more than able.

God had showed Caleb the grapes of the land and the possibilities of what he could have, so the giants really did not matter. You see Caleb was more focused on the promise than on the problem. He was an opportunity for a better life and he was will to fight if necessary in order to lay hold to a better quality of life. Let me caution you that there are always enemies to the promise that want to intimidate you and cause you to shriek back. They are geared to steal your courage and hope. That is why God had given them just a little glimpse of the grapes.

The Bible says that one cluster of grapes were so big until it took two people to carry them.

This land had promised to be more than enough for them and their children. The only thing that stood in the way of them was the fact that they did not believe that they could take it from the enemy. They had impossible thinking but Caleb had possibility thinking. The point that I am trying to make is through prayer and scripture reading you will develop a mind that is full of faith.

Caleb said let us go up at once and take the land. What he was saying is let us go out and take it right now. A possibility thinker moves out toward the goal without procrastination. Possibility thinkers are pathfinders, trailblazers, pace setters and they set the tone for success. Give them a problem and they will solve it. Possibility thinkers do not have to have every single fact before they move ahead. If they get a dream then they move on it.

They know that much will be discovered as the walk in the direction of the dream. They never allow fear to be their determining decision they program themselves to move against their fears. They do not resist new challenges and ideas neither do they have to follow the normal pattern of things. They are risk takers and they are not afraid to be creative and take chances.

The possibility thinker demands success even before they begin just as Caleb did. They never look for reasons why things cannot be done but they only look for ways to make things possible. Possibility thinkers never consider themselves to be at a disadvantage. Whatever the challenge they will meet it. Over the years, I have listened to people come up with many different reasons why they are not successful. When I examine all of these reasons none of they are valid. My desire is to take away your excuse to fail. Once you begin to honestly decide that you are willing to face your oppositions head on then you will truly know what the saying means when they say, "If there is a will then there is away." There is always a way just because you do not have it figured out yet; does not mean that it won't come in time.

EXCUSES THAT HINDER YOU FROM BECOMING A POSSIBILITY THINKER

I have a good idea but I do not have the money to fund it: Never allow you lack of finances to stop you from moving toward your dreams. If you go forth with perseverance then the money will come. Just get a solid plan.

I am too young or too old: Never allow age to be a determining factor for what you want in life. You have to look past age because if you are young enough or old enough to still dream then you can still achieve it.

I am the wrong color: There is really no such thing. Once you move toward the dream, opposition will come but you should never allow the thought to come into your mind that you cannot do it because of your skin color. Just push on and doors will open. There are people in this world who do not care what color your skin is.

I do not have enough time: You have got to be willing to make time for what is important. A little time may be one or two consistent hours a day is better than spending no time at all.

I come from a humble beginning: It does not matter where you come from only where you desire to go. There have been many people who have grown up in poverty-stricken environments that have gone on to accomplish great things. As a matter of fact, I would like to encourage you to allow your lack to push you into greatness.

I am not educated enough: There are two things that you can do about this. The first thing you can do is go back and get the required education that is needed. The next thing that you can do is develop your gifts, talents, and abilities to the degree that they bring profit and security to you. Education or lack of it cannot stop you from achieving your goals and dreams.

TROUBLE DOES NOT LAST BUT PEOPLE OF FAITH DO

Dear brothers and sisters, whenever trouble comes your way, let it be an opportunity for joy. For when faith is tested, your endurance has a chance to grow. So let it grow, for when your endurance is fully developed, you will be strong in character and ready for anything. James 1:2-4

Whenever trouble comes to the average person's life, they become confused as to how they should deal with it. This causes the majority of people to experience a lot of negative mixed emotions. Depending on the situation, many different things could go through the mind. Anything from anger, confusion, self-pity, hatred, and even sorrow. How you view life in times of trouble means a lot. It is not the trouble itself that matters as much as how you perceive it.

The above scripture says let your trouble become an opportunity for joy. How is this possible? Here it is you have all the troubles of this world bombarding you, so it seems. And the writer is saying in the mist of it all use it as an opportunity of Joy? Who gets happy and overwhelmed with excitement when they are faced with the storms of life?

Everything that happens in the human life regardless of how it looks at the present time can be altered and tweaked to work in your favor. Understanding the cause of a thing can change the fear, dread, and disappointment of it. There are a lot of people living in limbo and have given up on life because they did not understand why they were overwhelmed by trouble. Trouble does not always give off warning signs before it comes to you most of the times it comes by surprise.

We must come to the realization that life has a mixture of occurrences and events. Life graces us with peace sometimes and at other times, it whips us with chaos. Life can sometimes dazzle us with beauty and repel us with things that are hidden. And of course life brings us times of joy and bliss but it does throw us with times of trouble. But the beautiful truth of it all is both good and bad times are all a part of life.

Through both experiences if understood, we can learn a valuable lesson. The best times in your life are not the times of joy and laughter although they feel a whole lot better. But the best times are the painful times because it is in these times that we are challenged to grow. When things that normally discus hurt and break your spirit no longer have those effects on you then that means you have grown.

The scripture says that we are to let our troubles be an opportunity for joy. The problem is that most people experience the trouble but they never receive the benefit of the joy that follows it. For the believer trouble is only a faith enhancer. Just think no matter what we face or go through God still has our backs and best interest at hand that is the proper way to face trouble. Trouble simply means that I am getting ready to break into another level so that God can use me. A person who looks to always avoid trouble is a person who will stay immature in the Christian Faith. Trouble will either make you soldier up or back down. In order to be successful in life you have got to develop a high tolerance for opposition. Through this, we gain endurance.

Trouble has broken more people than the Cowboys of the Wild West broke horses. Once you go through your trouble there is always promotion.

In the mist of trouble sometimes, strength is lost. In these times, you must be willing to weather the storm by waiting it out. There come times when it seems as if no move is the right move; all you can do is be still.

In the process of waiting we, as Christians must look to God and in doing so he elevates

us according to Isaiah 40:31 but they that wait upon the Lord shall renew their strength; they shall mount up with wings as eagles; they shall run and not be weary; and they shall walk and not faint. (KJV)

Anticipating something great is up a head with an assurance that God is still in control is the power that our hope is rooted in. One of the things that we as the people of God must come to realize is that God would not bring us to it if He did not intend to bring us through it. Without life's challenges and difficulties there will be no growth. Sometimes when we as human beings are overwhelmed with hardship we allow our hearts to flutter with fear of the unbearable of life.

There are those things that have been locked into the mind of every person on the face

Of planet earth that they feel as if, they cannot handle it if it ever was to happen. There is a degree of trouble that can cause anyone to go into shock when it penetrates the life of individuals. Everyone's shock level is not the same. Some things that will send some people into shock may not necessarily affect others in the same way.

But the bottom line is men and women must be able to draw their source of hope and strength from a power that is greater than them. A brief moment of crises leaves a person powerless and without strength. The mere human makeup is not equipped to handle certain situations. God never intended for us to be totally independent but he wants us to become God dependent.

Your human strength and dependence will only take you so far. Those are some of the reasons that people face nervous breakdowns because they are trying to handle and carry all the weight of the world on their shoulders. What a great deceit for anyone to believe within themselves that they can handle everything that life throws at them. Throughout the years, I have heard people take credit for personal strength for their high achievements and ambitions when in fact it had more to do with self-discipline than it has to do with having a strong mind.

Any mentally sane person that has a strong relationship with God will be able to bear more and excel higher in life. The person who knows God as their strength will be able to conquer any obstacle that life puts in front of them. Anticipating God to move on your behalf is half the battle won in the mist of crisis. Crisis situations do not but it means it is time to go to your next level by looking unto God. The season of PUSH is what I like to refer to the troubled times that we face in life.

In this way, I like to equate trouble with birthing pains. Somewhat like a woman who is about to give birth to a newborn child. First, the contractions take place, then the water breaks, and then the cervix opens up, next comes the head of the baby. The whole entire process is very uncomfortable for the expecting mother but she realizes that this is something that she must endure if she is going to see the coming forth of New Life.

With every push she experiences another pain but it is all for a good purpose. This is how God has it sets up with the troubles of life they come and at times they bring us much discomfort but with God they help us to reach that next level they cause New Things to be firth forth in our lives. Anytime new

things are about to be birth in your life you will face some difficult times.

Do not allow those troubles to level you out but level you up. In other words, do not let troubles steal hopes, dreams, and visions that will cause there to be stagnation in your life. But allow it to put you in the expectations of God by waiting on the Lord. The word mount up in our scripture test is taken from the Hebrew word ALAH. It means to ascend and to be high to excel and exalt. Those who learn to wait upon the Lord will ascend, excel, and be exalted this is the promise that God has made us.

It does not matter how low in troubles and despair that you have found yourselves in

But once you learn that these troubles are only temporary then you do not mind waiting them out. Someone once said it I did not have any problems then I would not know that God could solve them I would not know what fate in His Word could do. It is all about trusting in the Lord no matter what the situation is.

There is a place in God that you can grow into that troubles will no longer cause you to lose momentum. You learn to run and not grow weary and you walk and do not faint. The trials of life will cause you to develop strength in areas that you never knew you could gain strength in. Sometimes you run and sometimes you walk but in both cases, you keep on moving forward. Storms and trials do not mean that you pray harder. The reason that most people pray harder in the mist of their troubles is that they are in panic and fear.

The goal is to relax and have faith. This is a principal that will forever change your life and circumstances. If you can learn to relax and breathe,

easy in the mist of your troubles leaning on an on and trusting God then that is the best thing that you can do for yourself. Let us take a look in the Bible and see how Jesus expects us to deal with the troubles and trials of life. Let us a look at the break down of

Mark 4:37-41 And there arose a great storm of wind and the waves beat into the ship, so that it was not full. And he (Jesus) was in the hinder part of the ship, asleep on a pillow: and they awake him, and say unto him, Master, carest thou not that we perish? And he arose, and rebuked the wind, and said unto the sea, Peace, be still. And the wind ceased, and there was a great calm. And he said unto them, Why are ye so fearful? How is it that ye have no faith? And they feared exceedingly, and said one to another, What manner of man is this, that even the wind and the sea obey him?

There arose a great storm. This was not just your average typical storm. This was one

That turned big strong men into wimpy cowards. The kind that would make you wish that you were any place else except in the mist of this type of trouble. This storm was brutal and heart wrenching. Everything in the natural circumstances looked to be hopeless.

The Bible lets us know that even the waves of the sea were going down in the mist of this overwhelming storm. The hearts of the disciples were perplexed and impacted with fear because their focus was on the problem instead of the problem solver. The fear of the surrounding storm and trouble had stolen their hearts with the confusion of fear. Any faith that they may have had was snatched away from them by the grip of terror.

It is very possible that they had gone through storms before but this was not just any storm but the Bible describes this as a great storm. This is what I call unusual, unexpected, and overwhelming trouble. Can you imagine yourself out on a ship enjoying yourself, loving life and soaking in the beautiful sunshine and then all of a sudden a life-threatening storm out of nowhere hits. These men did not have time to think up some faith. If the faith was not, there on the inside of them before the storm it surely was not going to manifest in the mist of it.

Although the problem quickly and suddenly arose, the problem solver was at ease in the back of the ship asleep on a pillow. The lesson here to be learned is no matter what trouble comes our way we must relax and trust that Jesus is in the storm with us. He never allowed the storm to move Him from His current position physically or mentally. On the other hand, the disciples were moved in both of these areas. They were running around like they had lost their minds in a fearful state of panic. But Jesus maintained His cool.

They had already embraced the vision of death. That is why they asked Jesus did He not care if they perish. The truth is Jesus did not care as a matter of fact Jesus did not have a care because He learned how to cast His cares upon God knowing that whatever He feared it was in the hands of God the

Father and that alone made everything alright. Now I already know what some people are thinking. You may be saying to yourself "Well Jesus was God and I am not."

What so many people do not realize is that Jesus laid down His divinity when He came to the earth and took on total humanity according to Philippians 2:6 & 7 This is why you always will see in the scriptures Him praying for the help of His

Heavenly Father. Everything that happened in the lives of these disciples while they were with Jesus was an opportunity for him to be an example to them on how they were to respond to life's' difficulties.

There were at least two different ways that Jesus could have dealt with the storm that He and His disciples had found themselves in. The first thing He could have done was remained asleep on a pillow. Meaning keep his head in comfort. Second, He could have done just what He did and that is take command over it and speak to it. Either way the promise of getting through their troubles were guaranteed.

No matter what you face, God has more than one way to get you out of your storm. No matter how impossible the situation seems. You will make it if you stay close to Jesus and keep your faith alive. Trouble does not last always but people of faith do.

THE LIFE THAT YOU ARE ENTITLED TO

The life that God wants you to live is a life that is above the average. Why is it that most people settle with less than Gods best for them? Life is meant to be lived to the fullest extinct. The only thing that can stop you from living that type of life is you. All of your failures and shortcomings is only in your own mind. All of those self-defeating thoughts that have held you back is where the problem is.

Once you start believing that because of your relationship with Jesus Christ you no longer have those defeating boundaries then and only then are you on your way to the life that is entitled to you.

John 10:10 Jesus says that He came that we might experience and abundant life. The Greek word for abundantly is PERISSEUO and it means to super abound (in quality or quantity) be in excess.

It also means to exceed, excel and to increase. The life that Jesus wants for you is one that will super abound. Wherever there is stagnation and hindrances in your life just know that, it is not the best life that God has for you. By following, His total plan for your life He will always gives you a life of quality and increase. It is impossible for a person to follow God's plan for their lives and not experience increase.

God does not have to back and support you plans but He does support the plan that He has for your life. Most people do not believe that God wants them to experience the type of live that most people only imagine. Gaining a mental picture in prayer of what God has in store for you will help you to obtain it. Sometimes getting out of the box of average is hard to do. This is why you must learn to go against the grain with courage. As I said in an earlier chapter once, you learn how to put away your fears of failure then you will be willing to become a risk taker.

We are only given one life here on earth and we are always at war trying to find peace, security, and happiness. For most people the bliss of life is far and in between. If Jesus indeed comes that you might have an abundant life then it is going to be in your constant connection with Him that you are going to experience it. You must come to the place in life where you refuse to settle with whatever comes your way.

No longer, should you just let life happen but you must make life happen. Become the captain of your own ship and the master of your life. God wants you to enjoy life. I Timothy 6:17 lets us know that God gives us richly all things for us to enjoy. Isn't it wonderful that God does not want to spoil your enjoyment? The only problem is most of the time our own self-seeking minds think that we know what will make us happy. Temporary gratification of the flesh will never make us satisfied. Yet these are the things that most people seek.

True happiness is found in the God things of life. To put it a better way they are found in the God plan for your life. Are you connected to God to the degree that you know what He wants you to do in this lifetime? This is how we find the abundant life that the scripture talks about in John 10:10. Outside of the will of God, you have an enemy who is known as the Devil and He will make sure that you do not enjoy life. This is the reason that He fights the minds of most people in order to keep them out of the plan of God.

Simply put He wants to make your life miserable. As we have explained in the last

Chapter that when you are in the plan and will of God even troubled times seem to somehow, work to your benefit. It has always been in the plan of the Lord to bring His

people into lands of increase and abundance. God wants to give the good things that the

Heathen nations enjoy to His people. Exodus 3:8 lets us get a glimpse of what God wants us

to enjoy the same way He intended for His first congregation. It says (and I am come down to deliver them out of the hand of the Egyptians, and to bring them up out of that land unto a good land and a large, unto a land flowing with milk and honey; unto the place of the Canaanites and the Hittites, and the Amorites and the Perizzites, and the Hivites, and the Jebusites).

This is the land also known as the Promised Land. That is because God had promised His people that once He delivered them from bondage that He would bring them into a greater inheritance. All of the things that people seek and even lose their souls for are easily obtained through a relationship and obedience to the will, purpose, and plan of God.

It is amazing how the unregenerate mind of the unbeliever buys into the lie that this world has the best things to offer. This is what I call the big deception even many Christians have become a victim to this type of mindset. The problem that most Christians face is they will not sacrifice momentary gratification for a greater good. A person, who is selfish and wants it all now, will do his or her own choosing and they will always end up with less than Gods best for their lives.

God had promised His people a promised land but He also told them that there would be enemies that were in that land that felt they had a legal right to it. You

have to understand that the land had been occupied for years by heathen, pagan god worshippers. They had been guarding and fighting so that they could keep the best of everything for themselves.

But God wanted there to be a transfer of wealth. And today it is no different. God wants His people to take back the wealth that the enemy of our souls have had possession of for so long. Our job is to reclaim the land and take back what the devil has stolen from us. Stop letting the devil tell you that he is the proper owner of the territory of your life. God owns everything and He has given it to His children now go and take it back.

CIRCUMSTANTIAL PEOPLE

You cannot become the type of person who is always moved by situations and circumstances. There are people who are really happy when things are going well. But when things as they will take a sudden unexpected twist for the worst their countenance quickly changes. Unless you allow yourself to grow to the place where you are not easily moved by circumstances then you will always be an under achiever in life.

This chapter is to encourage you to keep pushing forward no matter what it looks like in the natural. No matter what your ambition is in life it probably will not come to pass without a challenge or many challenges as far as that is concerned. You must become immune to difficult circumstances. This is truly the mark of a winner. As long as you are easily overwhelmed by the struggles of life then you will always live by your emotions. Living by emotions means that they will dictate to you your every move.

If the emotions are high and upbeat then you will excel and do good but when they are down then you will accomplish very little. Living by emotions is not good. You must learn how to excel and press forward no matter how you feel. As a matter of fact, that is what achieving success is all about. We must learn to press in even the more in the hard times because it is in those times that we see what we are made of. Unless a person learns how to stabilize their emotions then they will not excel in this life.

Let me show you how your emotions can ruin your whole days. Mark wakes up one morning and he hears the birds chirping outside of his window the beautiful sun light reflects through his window and he has a smile on his face. "This is going to be a beautiful day," he says to himself. As he walks down the stairs, he is warmly greeted by his dog Diamond with a

whole lot of tail wagging and doggie kisses. As he gets to the bottom of the stairs, he steps into doggie poop! "Diamond get in to your cage now!" he screams.

Now there is poop all over his brand new carpet. There has been a quick shift in his emotions. "Okay" he reasons within himself." I will just take a moment and clean this up and then I will head out to work he thought. He waste no time cleaning up the mess but at the same time, he is making himself furious by his own words. "That old stupid dog I know I should have gotten rid of him a long time ago." Mark said to himself. Finally, Mark gets finished cleaning the carpet. He looks over at the clock on the wall and he notices that he only has a few minutes to take his shower, eat breakfast, and get to work.

He rushes in and out of the shower puts two Pop Tarts into the toaster, pours himself a glass of milk, and makes a dash for the door. He thinks to himself "finally I am on my way to work." All of a sudden, he turns his key in the ignition but it does not start. "I cannot believe it this stupid car is only two years old." "God you must really love me because you chastise those who you love." He said very sharply and sarcastically.

His circumstances are continuing to get the best of him. So he gets out of the car and he pops the hood and checks the engine being very angry and hostile but he still cannot seem to diagnose the problem. At this point, he is screaming and cursing at the car with much vulgar profanity. So he sits down in the driver's seat while the hood of the car is up and he continues to talk to himself. "This has got to be the worst day of my Life." Finally, after thirty minutes of

griping and complaining he gets the thought "check the cables only to find them very lose.

He reaches under his seat, gets out a wrench, tightens them up gets back into the drivers' seat, and turns the key and right away, the car starts. Now he is even more furious than he was at first. Why didn't I check those battery cables at the start? "I have got to be the most stupid person in the world." He continues, "Now I am 45 minutes late for work." Mark gets to work late, he walks into the office, and he is met by his boss at the door. His boss chews him out before Mark has a chance to explain his reason for being late. Now his total day has been ruined. None of these events that took place were in his power to change.

These things just happened.

Now Mark is stressed out, he is angry, his blood pressure is up, and he is even blaming God for giving him such an awful day. Let us not forget when woke up life was beautiful but when he encountered adverse circumstances his heart, mind and over all thought process changed for the worst. Now he must wait until is circumstances change before his mood changes. This is why people get stuck because their emotions are tied into their circumstances.

Becoming a bag of emotions due to circumstances will keep you from walking in the freedom that wants you to walk in. We walk by faith not by sight (circumstances). Faith just keeps on telling you that it is going to be all right. Faith does not panic nor does it cause you to lose your cool. Each unfortunate event must be approached with the right attitude. A bad attitude in the mist of bad circumstances makes things twice as bad.

You have got to grab hold of your thoughts and make them submit to the way God wants you to

deal with every situation. II Corinthians 10:5 (KJV) says Casting down imaginations, and every high thing that exalteth itself against the knowledge of God, and bringing into captivity every thought to the obedience of Christ;

When our circumstances are gloomy, they cause our imaginations to run wild. If we are not careful those things that we imagine in the mist of bad circumstances will seem as if they over rule the Word of God. We cannot afford to allow things to exalt themselves over the Knowledge of God. In the mist of bad circumstances, we must get a grip on our thought process. We must change the mental pages in our minds quickly and make our thoughts line up with the thoughts of Christ.

You can always tell a circumstantial type of person. They are the type of people who go through many different mood swings depending on the circumstances. If things are good then they are happy if things are bad then they are bad. Everything is all about the circumstances. Circumstantial people are what the Bible calls being led by the flesh. They are people who base everything on what they see, feel, and experience in the natural.

These types of people operate in the perimeters of their own minds. They make conclusions before they even see the entirety of the matter. We must walk by faith and not by flesh. Your emotions belong to you they are yours. It is up to you to get a grip on them. The best way to do this is to trust in God and do not rely on your own understanding especially if your thoughts are negative ones.

There are two ways that you can deal with adverse circumstances. There is your way and then there is God's way. Doing it, your way will always

bring more regret. But discovering Gods way and then put it into action, it will always produce good benefits for your life. Whenever you find yourself faced with difficult circumstances, it is good to do these things.

Pray and ask God, how does He want you to deal with the challenge that is placed before you?

Refuse to let your emotions get overwhelmed by the circumstances.

Regrets the negative thoughts of fear.

Seek Godly counsel since there is a multitude of wisdom feared in it.

Realize that God has not brought you to something that he is not willing to bring you through.

Refuse to get a bad attitude.

Let positive confessions come out of your mouth.

Speak your desired out come into your situation.

Become the type of person who can function in the midst of adversity.

Do not let your circumstances lead you but you must remember that you are in control.

TAKE DOMINION OVER YOUR LIFE

And God said, Let us make man in our image, after our likeness; and let them have dominion...Genesis 1:26 (KJV)

Dominion in the Webster Dictionary describes it as having supreme authority and having absolute ownership. Every child owns what his good Father owns. Dominion is an extension of the image and likeness of God toward man. It is a gift that we must first realize that we have. Knowledge of this fact is empowerment. The deception of the devil that has destroyed the self-esteem of many people having them living beneath what God wants for them. His whole goal and plan is to keep you powerless.

A person is not worth much good to themselves and others when they live a defeated life. God put dominion inside man at the very onset of life. That is a part of what he put inside of mankind as His primary function. Do you believe that you have supreme authority and absolute ownership over everything in the earth realm except the mind and will of other people?

In order to take dominion we must also develop what I like to refer to as a dominant mind set. This means that we realize that we were made to be commanding, controlling, prevailing, and superior over all situations that we face. Nothing is too big or great that we cannot conquer. Dominion allows us through God to stay at the wheel of our lives. This dominion is in the sphere of our relationship with God through Jesus Christ.

The Bible says that we are seated with Jesus in heavenly places (Ephesians 4:6 KJV)

God wants us to overlook and command from a superior elevation. The place that we access this dominion is the heavenly realm from where we are seated. This relationship is formed out of the connection that we have with the Lord. If a man or woman can learn to take dominion over their thought process then they can take dominion over their life.

The only thing that can ever defeat you is the thing that is between both of your ears. Your Own Mind!

Being able to go outside of your comfort zone and face all of your fears head on is what allows you to walk in dominion. Many of us have discovered a place of comfort that has caused us to become under achievers. It is in the uncomfortable places that high achievers are made. In order to understand this principle we must become risk takers. We must learn how to except our God given inheritance and practice it in every area of our lives except when it comes down to dealing with other people. In the Book of Genesis, I want you to notice that God gave us dominion over everything except for other peoples wills. The will of man is an area that God Himself does not ever violate.

But all the things that God has placed under manpower we have a right to dominate over it. It is our attitude of acceptance of things as is that will not allow us to be relentless in our pursuits and endeavors. I would dare to say that mankind when connected to God has no limits and anything that he can think on and pray about he can achieve it.

All success comes from a power source and there is always spiritual influence and insight given from an unseen force. We as Christians draw our influence from God through Jesus Christ. Those who do not know God is receiving downloads of How To knowledge from the enemy of God. But it all comes from a power source. A tormented mind that is dominated with depression, struggles, and an inability to achieve is a self-sabotaging condition that has opposing unseen forces prompting those thoughts.

The Bible bares this statement out as fact in Ephesians 6:12 (KJV) which says For we wrestle not against flesh and blood, but against principalities,

against powers, against the rulers of the darkness of this world, against spiritual wickedness in high places.

The above scripture is talking about the unseen forces that come to control with us in every area of our lives. These forces keep us restrained and boxed in if we do not use our God given authority in order to push them back and open up new doors of opportunity. Evil spirits are those unseen powers that bring frustration to the lives of believers as well as those who do not.

Once you learn how to take dominion in the Spirit realm then your natural world begins to line up for the better. There is such a thing as a moving back the dark forces that come to torment the lives of the people of God. Now am I saying that Christians will never have any struggles or problems? Of course not! But what I am saying is to the degree that the Holy Spirit reveals to you over and over that there is a better inheritance than we must go for Gods best and not settle for less.

Believe it or not, just as God is concerned with getting all manner of good things into your life the devil is bent on bringing all kinds of frustrations and chaos into your life. His plan is to close you in on every side with sickness, poverty, low self-esteem, low self-worth and anything else he can use to keep you powerless and a puppet on his string. Many have accepted the lie that says living in defeat is in the plan of God.

Yet nobody has been able to prove it scripturally. Scripture speaks of the plan of Satan to try to stop us from living in and doing the Will of God for our lives. And sometimes Satan

does hinder us. Let me back up the above statement by the words of the Apostle Paul.

Wherefore we would have come unto you, even I Paul, once and again; but Satan hindered us. I Thessalonians 2:18 (KJV)

It is impossible for me to talk about becoming successful Gods way in the natural without going behind the wall of the Spiritual. There are two forms of success. There is the real form of success from God and there is the false form that snatches the very Soul out of a man or woman that comes from the enemy of God.

If you do not have a trained eye as to what you are looking at then you will not know

How to distinguish between the two of them. This is why so many Christians have found themselves shipwrecked because they wanted to touch the world's form of success, which always has a great price connected to it.

Now when I am talking about success in life I am not just talking about making a lot of money this is indeed the world's idea of it. But what I am talking about is well-rounded success that includes financial blessings but it is not limited to it. I submit to you that there are many different people who are miserable with money. They have never learned how to take the God given dominion over their lives especially in the areas of the mind will and the emotions.

A lot of money in the hands of an unhealthy spiritual person can only be dangerous to themselves

173

as well as others. Evil spirits have in many cases been the distributors and the withholders of wealth. These two Spirits among many are found in the scripture in Malachi 3:11 speaks of a spirit that is called the Devourer. The word literally means to eat and to consume. There is a spirit that has an assignment to eat up your money and resources.

The next evil spirit we are going to talk about is found in Acts 16:16. The Bible calls it the spirit of Divination in the Greek language it is known as the Phantom in the English translated to be Python. The Bible says that this spirit brought her masters much gain. This is what we find operating in the arenas of the worldly success especially in the entertainment business.

The Python is known as a constrictor and its job is to bring wealth at the expense of choking the life out of others. Entertainers make millions and millions of dollars through rap music, acting, rock music and many other different sources but look at the overall effect that it is having on the masses as a whole. It is literally suffocating the life out of our society. We must take dominion over these Spirits and embrace the blessings of God. There is never sorrow although we will live in this natural realm everything is ultimately controlled by the spiritual realm.

Thoughts, ideas, passions, and mindsets are all spiritual and every one of these has influence from another source. I do not care who a person is if the President of the United States or a Farmer down in Utah somewhere in their minds is not controlled by the influence of the Spirit of God then that person is not free to succeed into the God kind of success. When we keep our eyes on this world's form of success then we become carnal.

Carnality has invaded the church in such a way that we can no longer accept the self-defeating thoughts of worldliness. Take dominion in the Spiritual Realm by Prayer and change your natural realm in every way.

GETTING THE REAL BLESSINGS ON YOUR LIFE

Now the Lord had said unto Abram, Get thee out of thy country, and from thy kindred, and from thy father's house, unto a land that I will shew thee: And I will make of thee a great nation, and I will bless thee, and make thy name great; and thou shalt be a blessing: Genesis 12:1 & 2 (KJV)

And Abram went up out of Egypt, he, and his wife, and all that he had, and Lot with him, into the south. And Abram was very rich in cattle, in silver, and in gold. Genesis13:1 & 2 (KJV)

The word Blessing in the Hebrew language is BARAK. It is the gift of divine favor that prevents misfortunes and releases special benefits upon the life. It also means a special endowment to prosper. This is what every man or woman that is a child of God should want on their life. One may ask the question "how do I get the blessing on my life"? The true blessing always comes as a result of total obedience to the Word of God.

In the scriptures above you see that God asked Abram who later became Abraham to get away from everybody and everything that he was familiar with and journey into unfamiliar territory. Abraham had to obey God and get away from the people who possibly had influence on him so that he would be free to obey God. Separation from the opinions of men is very necessary when it comes down to being led by God into the place of Blessing.

Some of the people who have your best interest at hand either limit your potential to succeed or out of fear of you failing try to protect you by suggesting that you make only safe moves. But God commanded Abram to make a blind move and to get away from the people who he knew so that he could bless him. The man or woman who will be blessed of God will embrace the divine separation of God.

God wants to raise a people up to be his billboard of blessings. He wants to display you before the world so that the heathen will know that there is no God like Jehovah. Even as God promised that, He would make Abrams name great it is the same thing that he wants for your name. But before God can do this for you, He has to purge you from rebellion and a disobedient heart. A rebellious person will only end up squandering the blessings and making a mockery of

God. There is no fast track or self-exaltation into the blessings. The secret is to remain obedient to the Word and Will of God and the blessings will follow. Satan the enemy of God has made many of His follower's names great. The reason He does this is because he realizes that a great name has influence. Look at all of the Hip Hop Artist, Actors, Rock n Roll groups and the countless others who promote Satan's' agenda in the earth realm. They gather to themselves many followers who pattern themselves after them.

God wants His people to out shine the kingdom of darkness. Everything that the kingdom of this world produces ends in sorrow and regret. I do not care how it starts out it always ends up in misery. A totally surrendered life to the Lord will always release blessings to flow into your life. A person who walks in the blessings of God is not affected by the problems that overwhelm other people.

Abram was in a land that was overtaken by a famine but because of the blessing that was on his life he walked out of it, the Bible says very rich in material goods. The blessing of God is always accompanied by outward manifestations but is not limited to it. The New Testament describes the blessing as influence upon the emotions. It defines the blessing as happy. The false blessing can give you some things that you have desired but it does not produce satisfaction to the Heart and Soul of man.

Even as the blessings made Abram rich, the blessings will make you rich to the degree that you can enjoy them. Proverbs 10:22 lets us know, the blessings of the Lord, it maketh rich, and he addeth no sorrow with it. Many people are claiming the fact that they are blessed but at the same time, they are always in a sorrowful state of mind. Out of all, that we have written about in this book there is nothing

that can out do the blessed life. The blessing even affects your children, children for the better.

And it shall come to pass, if thou shalt hearken diligently unto the voice of the Lord thy God, to observe and to do all his commandments which I command thee this day, that the Lord thy God will set thee on high above all nations of the earth: And all these blessings shall come on thee, and overtake thee, if thou shalt hearken unto the voice of the Lord thy God. Blessed shalt thou be in the city, and blessed shalt thou be in the field. Blessed shall be the fruit of thy cattle, the increase of thy kine, and the flocks of thy sheep. Deuteronomy 28:1-4 (KJV)

And the Lord shall make thee plenteous in goods, in the fruit of thy body, and in the fruit of thy cattle, and in the fruit of thy ground, in the land, which the Lord swore unto thy fathers to give thee. Deuteronomy 28:11 (KJV)

Notice the pattern of the blessing and how it is obtained; it always starts with obedience to the Lord. The benefit is always making the person who is blessed great. In the above scriptures, it speaks about setting your name on high. This means to be recognized as one who is blessed by God. The blessing will overtake you. This is a wonderful place to be in when the Divine Favor of God just keep on coming upon you when you least expect it.

The blessing is not limited to a geographical location. If you are in the city or the field the blessing will meet you wherever you go. Only in a committed life to obey God can you experience such a blessing. If you want to change the disaster of your family lineage then it will start with your obedience. The scripture says that even the Fruit of your body will be blessed. The favor that is upon you will also rest upon your children.

So many times, we have witnessed a family that seems like they prosper in everything that they do. Whenever you see such a favorable people it is only because someone in that

Family tree lived up right before God. Many people are not willing to put away their former ways and follow His will. This is why so many believers do not know what it is to experience God's best for their lives. It all begins with a willing and determined heart. Going against the desires of God for your life will only bring curses upon you and your family. You do not have the answers or the blue print for the blessing written yourself. It has to be discovered through the knowledge that God gives to you.

The path that His Word leads you to is the path of the blessing. Our plans and agendas of the self-life will continue to detour you down the never-ending roads of hard ship, heartache, and pain. This means we must learn to trust that God knows what is best for us. Psalm 31:8 says blessed is the man that trusteth in the Lord. Following God is walking on the Blessed Path.

THE GOD KIND OF PROSPERITY IS AN EXTENTION OF THE BLESSINGS

This book of the law shall not depart out of thy mouth; but thou shalt meditate therein day and night, that thou mayest observe to do according to all that is written therein: for then thou shalt make thy way prosperous, and then thou shalt have good success. Joshua 1:8 (KJV)

If you notice, the above scripture that leads to prosperity is the same method that is used to get the blessing on your life. I believe that the blessing automatically brings prosperity. After all the definition of blessing is an endowment to prosper. It is very heart wrenching to see Christians struggling to live from day to day simply because they believe that prosperity is evil. But the truth is if we keep God's word in our mouths and meditate on it in our hearts with a desire to obey it then we make our own way prosperous.

This means that prosperity is a choice based on our own decisions. We must purpose in our hearts that we must be willing to sacrifice monetary gratifications and pleasures of sin in order to experience long term blessings, that can even effect the lives of your children's children. The blessing is how we gain success God's way. May we receive all that He has for us?

NINE KEYS TO EXPERIENCING THE BLESSED LIFE

Be willing and obedient to the Word of God. It is not just enough to be willing but you must also make a sincere effort to obey God's Word. Even so it is not enough just to be obedient you must develop a willing heart as well.

Meditate in God's Word. This will help you with your obedience and willingness. It is impossible to spend long periods of time in the Word and not change your ways.

Refuse opportunities for sin. I am convinced that the devil tries to make us continue in sin so that he can steal our blessings.

Be willing to embrace divine separation and get God's direction and not that of the people who have influence in our lives.

Be willing to let God purge you from disobedience through the Word and Prayer.

Refuse the self-life. Many of us have been our own boss and have done our own thing and we have tried to put God in it. Now we must adopt God's will, purpose, and plan for our lives.

Live a life totally surrendered to the Lord.

Learn to trust in God even when you do not understand what it is that He is doing.

Sacrifice momentary gratification for long-term blessings. The very mind set of resisting temptations in order to gain and maintain the blessing is important.

OBTAINING WEALTH

But thou shalt remember the Lord thy God: for it is, he that giveth thee power to get wealth that he may establish his covenant which he sware unto thy fathers, as it is this day. Deuteronomy 8:18 (KJV)

The Bible is the true intent of how God wanted and still desires life to be for His children. We need to know and understand that we have double the scriptures the Old Testament as well as the New Testament writers had to look in to. The point that I am trying to make is that we can see that God is not to be conformed to only on train of thought.

We should not try to box Him in to fit our own ideas of Him. This chapter is for all of them who are so sure that God and money, wealth and prosperity do not collaborate together. Some people want to use Jesus to separate the nature, intent, and desire of what God really wants for us. But the truth is Jesus came to display the character of God the Father to us. So when people say things like show me in the New Testament about prosperity and wealth it is based upon ignorance.

No matter how you look at it, the Bible is one book in its entirety from one Mastermind, which is God. In other words, all 66 Books really make one Bible from the Heart of One God. Just because some people have abused the prosperity message does not mean that I have a right to overlook it or discredit it. Along with the other demonic forces that promote their version of wealth, our God has a true version of it.

This is the message that I will promote throughout this chapter. When the world thinks of wealth, they only think of having more than enough resources for themselves. They are concerned with getting all that they can so appease their own sinful desires and agendas. But the wealth of God has always been given to His servants to display God and His will in the earth realm.

This is why I saved this chapter for the end of the book because I wanted to work on the things first

that is needed to maintain it once you get it. My overall plan was to set up for success. I have made an earnest attempt to take you through a process that will prepare the Heart for what God wants to do with you. We are the people who should control and distribute the wealth. We should be the main source that people run to when they need jobs.

And employment. Yes! God's people are the resource that the world needs to look to for help.

Please realize that the money belongs to God and it is not for your selfishness but for the display of a good God towards His people. If you can already see yourself in a Lear Jet, living in a big mansion and driving a Rolls Royce so that you can become something fantastic and stoke your ego then you truly have a wrong concept about wealth. This is not a message that is geared to appease your flesh, which will eventually lead to self-destruction. I want you to become someone who is humble enough so that God can trust you to become a distribution center for God.

In order to enjoy wealth one must remain grounded. I am convinced that the reason that God does not give most people wealth is because they are not spiritual enough to handle it. All of the evil things that men can only think about doing without money, with it they can now do. This is why the heart must be made right first. That point alone points out the difference between God's wealth system and the Devils.

The devil will open doors to obtain wealth no matter what the condition of your heart. As a matter of fact, he prefers your heart to be distorted. There are people who have never served God and they are worth billions of dollars. From the worlds definition of wealth this would be considered to be extremely wealthy. But most people who has all of this material

stuff and money but the seat of their heart is not committed to God, they are not happy. These people are not experiencing the whole life. You may even look upon these people to admire them and want to be like them because of what you see as a form of success.

But the truth is a heart that is separated from God is a life that is most miserable. Everything is about the power to choose. We can either take the time to find out God's way of living and obtaining wealth or we can keep on doing it our own way.

The Bible says it is God that gives us the power to get wealth. In the presence of God, he begins to download His thoughts and ways into our minds and it is in following them that we find ourselves in a wealth place.

We must understand that wealth is a part of the covenant blessings of God. In the Bible Covenant was one of the highest forms of agreement that two people or more could make. This agreement always made two separate people eternally become one. All that the one person owned became the equal possession of the other. In other words, all that God has is now yours when you understand covenant. His wealth is now your wealth. God is establishing His covenant by giving you the ability to get wealth.

Made in the USA
Charleston, SC
10 August 2014